SANCTUARY

League of Vampires

RYE BREWER

Cover Art by www.mirellasantana.deviantart.com
with Model Mirish – Deviant Art

SANCTUARY

A half-blood by birth.

Anissa Garnet is half-fae, half-vampire. And she's not the daughter of just any fae, she's the daughter of Gregor, the leader of the fae. Except now she's made the mistake of walking away from her fae kind.

As if that wasn't bad enough, she left her mother's kind—vampires—behind.

Now this half-breed has gone rogue, but she hasn't done it alone.

Vampire clan leader no more.

Jonah Bourke not only stepped down from being a clan leader, he also left behind his entire clan, the one he was destined to rule. All to merge his fate with Anissa, the slayer that had been sent to kill him.

New Alliances, old foes.

The Sanctum provides more than sanctuary. It provides answers, which sometimes leads to more questions, and then even more threats.

☙❧

Cover Art by

www.mirellasantana.deviantart.com

with Model Mirish – Deviant Art

JONAH

I couldn't believe I'd gone so far for so long, I'd fought to hold on to what my father left behind, when it came between me and my twin, I'd always been sure that my sitting at the head of the clan was what right and meant to be. Who was I to go against tradition?

Yet, here I was, only minutes earlier, renouncing what had been mine since birth.

I was sure, as I left the site of the League of Vampires meeting with Anissa's hand still in mine, I'd never forget the looks on the faces of everyone around me when I stood up and announced I was leaving. Scott, Philippa—they'd both looked ill. Philippa, especially. I'd been sure she'd jump on me, hold me down, fight to keep me there. But she hadn't. Maybe she'd been too stunned to move. Or maybe she'd known better than to think she could stop me. That was always possible. She did know me well.

For the briefest of brief moments, I was sure Marcus had thought he'd won. He couldn't have been more wrong. The clan was still in the hands of the Bourkes, and I'd waited long enough to be sure the terms of our boundaries were firmly in place before stepping down. I wasn't a fool, the way he thought I was. Though, who knew? I had walked away, after all. Maybe I was a bigger fool than I wanted to admit.

No. I wasn't. Because I had Anissa. I couldn't imagine going the rest of my existence without her. Maybe it was looking at Lucian, the most ancient of our kind, that made up my mind for me. Knowing I could live as long as him, without her.

Unthinkable. So very unfathomable.

In the face of something like that, how could I have chosen otherwise?

"Where are we going?" Anissa asked as we sped away from the cathedral.

I didn't want to course, that special means of travel we vampires had that took us from one location to another, very far away. That traveling method which drained us to the point of needing time to recuperate, being unable to fight, or course again, or even run. I didn't want to course because I wasn't sure what we'd face on our way to our destination and didn't want to tire us out, but it was important for us to move in a hurry. Like run.

"You'll see," I assured her. "Don't worry about anything. I have it all under control."

"You didn't plan this out, did you?" She gave me her slight smile, the crooked one, the one that made me want to press my lips to hers.

"No, I didn't," I admitted "But it's always good to have a Plan B. Part of being an effective leader and all."

It seemed so crazy, and I could tell she felt the same. We had gone against tradition, both of us, and we'd lived to tell the tale. I hoped she wouldn't regret it. I knew I never would, no matter what happened.

We stopped to rest for a minute at the border between New York and Vermont. From there, we would move farther east. Anissa looked around, still smiling.

"What's up?" I asked.

All I could see was a forest—a beautiful one, granted, but one like any other. So, why was she like that?

"It's gorgeous. I've always wanted to spend time exploring places like this," she confessed. "I guess it's in my blood. I never knew until now that it's because of my fae heritage, but since I found out, so many things make sense. Ironic that I spent my life so far in a world of glass and concrete."

"I wish we were here to explore," I apologized, "but we have to keep moving."

"Oh, I know. I'm just glad to see it with my own eyes instead of looking at pictures." Her golden eyes glowed. I couldn't help pulling her to me for a quick kiss. I had to be close to her, if only for a minute.

The sound of rustling not far from where we stood cut our minute short. We both froze, our instincts kicking into overdrive.

I held my breath while listening for more noise. Whatever had made those sounds in the brush was bigger than a deer, for sure. I wondered if it was the time of year for bears to go exploring—not that I couldn't take down a bear, but the surprise wasn't welcome.

Only, it wasn't a bear. I could smell the blood flowing through the body of the humans not far from us.

Anissa's eyes shifted up to mine, and I knew she could smell it, too.

Enforcers. Humans who were part of the Enforcer Coalition. A coalition with the sole purpose of deleting our kind.

They were taking their time about showing themselves, which meant they weren't out for a quiet stroll through the woods. They'd been stalking us.

"What are we going to do?" Anissa asked, only moving her mouth enough for me to read her lips.

We don't leave Enforcers alive. It's not prudent. The Enforcer we don't kill today could be the one that would kill us tomorrow. Plus, I couldn't afford to have them following us to the place we were going.

"Fight," I replied. She nodded, her expression hardening. Her skills would come in handy as would my strength.

We decided not a moment too soon because, in a flash, a

group of Enforcers surrounded us. They weren't like normal humans. They made taking down vampires their business.

Anissa groaned when she recognized them for who they were.

"Back off." I glared at them each in turn.

They looked like what humans referred to as hillbillies. Grimy faces, clothing that looked like it had been around for about as long as I had. But Enforcers were deceptive. They couldn't be judged on their looks alone. They were usually smart as whips, and fast. And strong. They trained in the art of killing vampires for years before being set loose on the population.

"You don't get to tell us what to do, vampire boy," the tallest one growled.

"There's a treaty between the humans and the vampires that stretches back decades," Anissa said.

I was proud when I heard the strength and confidence in her voice. She wouldn't let them know she was terrified, even though I could feel fear coming off her in waves. She stood with her back to my front, pressing herself against me.

I liked her spunk, thinking she could protect me. *That's my job,* I wanted to say.

"We don't care about treaties," another one of them spat. He held a crossbow. A crossbow, for the love of all that was good. They didn't have the money for clean clothing, but they could afford weapons.

"You're breaking your own laws," she continued, her head going back and forth as mine did, sizing up the group.

They closed in on us one step at a time, bloodlust in their eyes.

"Just let us go on our way, and there won't be any trouble." I turned with a start when I sensed one of them advancing on me from behind—a woman holding a spear jumped back.

"Sorry, you soulless blood sucker. We don't take orders from the likes of you."

They charged us.

Everything went by in a flash. I kicked out at the woman with the spear, hitting her in the sternum and sending her into a tree where she landed in a motionless heap. Then a smaller man ran at me, swinging a rope over his head like a lasso.

I grabbed for the loop, using it to pull him to me, instead. He screamed in terror when I bared my fangs. I threw him away from me with both hands, hitting another Enforcer with his body. They landed on their backs and were smart enough to stay on the ground.

Meanwhile, out of the corner of my eye, I saw Anissa sidestepping a swing from a man twice her size. She was quick as lightning, ducking, dodging, then somehow ending up on the man's back with her arms over his face. He was blind, flailing around with his arms waving. I didn't see what she did to him, but I heard the thump as he hit the ground.

I threw myself over Anissa, protecting her before barreling into the smallest of the group. He went head over heels, sprawled out to the side, and I ran for it. I heard them screaming behind me, then the sound of something zipping past my head. An arrow lodged itself in a tree trunk not a foot from me.

"We have to course!" I shouted, ducking behind a thick tree. "Are you ready?"

"If it means getting out of here, yes!" she screamed back.

"Follow me!"

And we were off, leaving the Enforcers and the woods behind us. I had gotten away with nothing more than a few scratches, while Anissa looked completely unharmed. I would have to ask her to teach me a thing or two about fighting if we ever got the time. It seemed like we were always too busy facing down enemies to do things like that.

I headed east, through the woods and into the mountains.

There was only one place I could take us.

We would be safe there. It wasn't an easy decision, but as we fled from our would-be murderers, it was the right one.

2

ANISSA

I hardly had time to catch my breath before we were narrowly avoiding death.

Then, as suddenly as we'd started, we stopped.

"Sorry," he said, catching me by the arms before I slammed into him. "I should have let you know. Only, I almost missed the spot."

"What spot?" I glanced around and saw nothing but mountains. Granted, it was beautiful, but there was nothing nearby that stood out as a landmark. I turned in a slow circle, trying to understand what he was talking about.

"You won't see it," he said with a chuckle. "Trust me. I almost missed it, and I know what to look for. You could stay out here for a year and not find it by accident."

Must be like the fae portal is for him, impossible to see.

But what would that be? What could it be? Frustration mounted in me. "Stop with all the riddles and just tell me what we're doing here," I said, slightly exasperated.

I still trusted him, but I was hardly in the mood for games. I had killed a human back there, something I didn't normally do. And we'd had a close call, no matter how one-sided the fight had seemed. Was that what we had to look forward to together? Nonstop fighting for our lives?

I glanced down at myself, groaning at what had become of Philippa's pretty dress after the fight. "At least I wore flats," I muttered, brushing what dirt I could off myself.

"Come on. I'm sure you can change into something more comfortable." He took me by the hand, leading me to a small brook.

"Change where?" I asked, still missing the big secret. "I don't see anything."

Then, to my surprise, he kept walking. He led me into the water. No, not into the water. Over the water. It only seemed like there was no bridge there, because it was nearly invisible.

"It's enchanted!" I breathed, gaping in surprise as I watched the world pass beneath my feet.

It wasn't a long bridge or a very tall one, but it spanned the brook and led through a grove of trees to a sheer rock face. The sight of Jonah pressing his palm against the smooth rock, then through it, took my breath away completely.

"What did you just do?" Then it came to me. The rock wall was an optical illusion. It was actually the entrance to a cave. We were only walking through the entrance, but the way the rock had been carved out, it appeared solid to the unknowing eye. I could understand what Jonah meant about never being able to un-see it after that.

"All right. Where are we?" I asked.

"You're one of the few of your kind who has ever stepped foot inside our territory," someone else said.

I jumped when I heard the voice to my right.

A tall, robbed figure stepped out of the shadows. I couldn't make out a face, thanks to the hood which concealed everything about the creature who'd spoken.

"Steward," Jonah said, a smile in his voice. "I'm so glad to see you."

"I wish I could say the same," Steward said. "I guess things didn't go well out there."

"Your guess is right." Jonah turned to me. "Like I said, this was always Plan B. But nobody wants to fall back on Plan B if hey can help it."

"This should be Plan Z. Last plan. Not the second option," Steward said.

"I don't understand," I murmured. "I'm sorry if I sound ungrateful, but where are we, exactly?"

Jonah cleared his throat. "Anissa, this is Steward. He's a friend of mine. The head of the Custodians."

I bit my tongue against the gasp threatening to escape. I felt very cold, all of a sudden. A Custodian? They were the sort of creature children heard stories about. Rumors. Heard of. Never seen. Like trolls, only they lurked underground. Or so I'd thought.

Were we underground? I didn't know what to say. Jonah had taken me to the one group considered completely off-limits to vampires—and vice versa, as Custodians were to never, ever show themselves in the vampire world. It could mean death.

"Come." Steward's voice was gravely, deep, and I didn't dare drag my feet. A Custodian. I'd never seen one in person, naturally. I didn't know what to expect. The size didn't surprise me. I knew they were supposed to be tall. Of course, when you're as short as I am, almost anyone is considered tall.

It was the robe that worried me—or, rather, the thought of what was underneath the robe. I couldn't see an inch of skin—even the sleeves fell way below his hands. There were all sorts of rumors as to what Custodians really were. Mutants, crossbreeds, anything and everything the imagination could dream up. Part-human... maybe. There was no way of knowing, and I wasn't about to ask.

Jonah's hand was strong and sure in mine, so I chose to go along with him. I didn't have a choice, really—it was either follow the Custodian into a series of underground tunnels or be left to an uncertain and probably very short life in the outside world.

Torches mounted along the walls lit our way as Steward led us deeper and deeper into the maze of passageways. I sensed the slight downward grade of the floor, telling me we were moving farther underground all the time. Although I was still half-terrified of the Custodian—and the thought there were more like him where we were headed—it was reassuring to know we'd be out of our enemies' clutches.

"It was Steward who first clued me in to the secret tunnel on the grounds of the Carver mansion," Jonah explained.

"Thank you for that," I said, speaking to the figure ahead of me.

"It's our job," he explained. "We're the keepers of knowledge and lore. The entire history of the vampire race can be found in our records. We've been keeping the archives for centuries."

I looked around, noticing the farther we got into the underground lair, the more openings I saw in the walls. They led to rooms, of course. I caught glimpses of scrolls in those rooms, and books. I could only imagine the wealth of knowledge the Custodians oversaw.

I shivered a little, which was strange since my kind rarely felt cold.

Jonah noticed. "Are you all right?"

"Are you cold?" Steward asked, not turning around.

"Yes, a little."

"It's normal," he said. "Most humans would get hypothermia down here in not much time at all. It's well below freezing. To you, it's just a little cold."

"Do you think you have any clothing she could wear?" Jonah asked.

"We have chambers. There are articles of clothing inside."

Great. I hoped it wasn't one of his robes. There's no way I'd fit in it. As long as they were warm, I guessed it didn't really matter.

I couldn't imagine living down here in the dank darkness. No matter how much lit torches, there was never enough light. It was still dark, gloomy, and cold. I hoped there would be a fire in my chambers.

Steward stopped, and I guessed we'd reached our destination.

Jonah stepped in front of him. "You don't know how grateful I am you've welcomed us here."

"I told you I'd always be here for you," Steward replied.

"Still, it means a lot."

"We're safe here—nobody knows how to find us."

I could believe that, since I never would have found the bridge or the entrance on my own. Besides, I thought, it would take more than a little courage to venture in here alone. We didn't have to worry about our enemies here, or my predators.

I entered one room, Jonah took a door leading to another. Somebody had gone to the trouble of setting out a wardrobe full of jeans, sweaters, and boots. I would be warm, thankfully. I wasted no time washing up, using the basin on the bedside table, then changing into decent clothes.

Then, I knocked at the door next to mine. Jonah stepped out in clean clothes. We looked at each other for a long time before I spoke.

"Custodians, huh?"

"It was the only logical choice."

"I'm not questioning your choice," I said with a grin. "I'm only wondering what other surprises you have up your sleeve."

He grinned back, and, for the first time since rescuing him from Marcus, I felt him relax.

Safe, for now. Maybe.

❧ 3 ❧

ANISSA

I t felt good to be safe, to be clean and comfortable—to an extent. To the furthest extent we could be, considering we were in an underground cave. Or a series of caves, maybe.

Vampire eyes are stronger than human eyes, naturally, and it was easy for me to adjust to the darkness. While the Custodians did their best, lighting the halls with torches, the entire underground system of hallways and rooms was cloaked in darkness. It made me wonder how anyone had ever managed in the days before electricity.

I glanced at Jonah, standing beside me in the hall as we waited for Steward to fetch us. He looked more beautiful than ever to me, which hardly seemed possible considering how crazy I already was about him. Beautiful seemed like such a strange word to use to describe him, but I couldn't think of any other. He was sheer perfection. Inside and out.

He'd given everything up for me. He'd already taken huge chances, and then he'd given up his birthright. I knew how important it was to him, leading his clan. He was proud of them. What did that say about his feelings for me? It was overwhelming, but the nice kind of overwhelming. The kind that made my heart beat fast and my palms all sweaty. I'd never felt this way before, though I'd always heard it was possible.

The appearance of Steward, nearly gliding down the hall in his hooded robe, pushed all thoughts of romance out of my head. I still wasn't completely sure about him, but Jonah trusted him. Besides, he'd saved us. I had to give him a chance—and, with that in mind, I smiled.

"I take it you're both comfortable?" Steward asked in that gravelly voice of his.

"Very. Thank you." I was far from comfortable, in reality, but it would be rude to voice my discomfort. Sure, the heavy cable knit sweater and fleece-lined jeans I wore helped with the incessant, bone-deep cold. I couldn't relax with being underground. I'd already seen so many unfamiliar places in such a short time. It was a lot to absorb. Being in a cold, dank underground lair was another surprise to adjust to.

"And you're certain you didn't lead anyone else here?" Steward asked Jonah as we walked.

I stayed one step behind. It was easier to look around, open-mouthed, when Steward's eyes weren't on me. The sheer size of the caves, the scope, made me wonder how long it had taken to create them. It was breathtaking.

"I'm sure," Jonah said. "The humans couldn't have caught up with us. And there were no vampires, fae, or anything else on our track."

The mention of vampires got me thinking. "What about Sara?"

Jonah and Steward stopped, turning to me.

"Who?" Steward asked.

"My sister." I looked at Jonah. "I should've thought about her. Oh, no."

The cold seeped through my clothes, making me shiver. Or maybe it was the mental image of my sister's torture. What if she suffered that again because I wasn't there to protect her? My thoughts spiraled out of control.

"Relax." Jonah's hands cupped my shoulders. "Scott will take care of her. He won't let anything bad happen."

I wanted so much to believe him. I told myself I had no choice but to believe him. When I remembered the way Scott had looked at my sister, I did believe. He wouldn't let her fall into the wrong hands.

Jonah waited until I met his gaze before speaking again. His eyes burned into mine. "You can't protect everybody, you know. You can't fight everybody's fights."

"But she started it," I whispered with a half-smile, what with her selling her blood and all that. But her reasons had been pure. She'd been trying to help me. I knew that. I hoped Jonah realized it, too. "She was the one who took chances for me."

"And that was her choice. It doesn't mean you have to jeopardize or punish yourself." His hands squeezed my shoulders. "You'll be all right, and so will she."

I felt better. His words and his touch were magic. "Okay." I nodded, determined to believe him, hoping he was right.

We continued on.

Steward remained ominously silent. What did he think of me, really? Was I a nuisance? I was an outsider. It was clear he wasn't comfortable with my being here—if anything, his friendship with Jonah was the only thing keeping me in his presence.

What did he look like under that hood?

"What is this place?" I asked, hoping to draw him into a story.

Maybe he'd be more comfortable if he talked about history—after all, he was a Custodian.

I continued, still wanting to make him feel at ease. "It's fascinating. To think, all of this exists without the knowledge of the rest of the world. How is it possible? I mean, granted, it's hidden very well."

"Yes, that's generally what we strive for," Steward replied, and I wondered if that was his idea of a little humor. It had sounded as though he'd tried to chuckle. "However, what most works in our favor is the fact we rely on the discretion of those who know of our existence."

"Understood," I said as we walked.

So, he was reminding me to keep my mouth shut.

Well, there was no problem with that. I didn't want to betray his confidence.

We walked through a doorway carved into the rock and stepped into a room which reminded me of a railroad terminal. I'd visited a few in my day. The ceiling was many stories up, and into the walls had been carved rows on rows stretching from the floor all the way to the top—I had to crane my neck to get a view of what was up there.

Walkways lined the walls, allowing Custodians to come and go. There weren't any around at the moment. Was everybody else sleeping? Maybe they slept during the day to avoid detection.

"It's magnificent," I breathed. Books. Books and books and scrolls and more books. I imagined having all that knowledge, all that history, at my fingertips. History was one thing I'd always excelled at in school.

"This is where we store most of the knowledge that's come into our hands over the centuries," Steward explained. "In the beginning, this place was called the Sanctum. That was many centuries ago. Now, it's referred to as the Sanctuary."

His words seeped into my consciousness as I looked around with wide eyes, still a little thunderstruck. "Sanctuary? Sanctuary for what?"

"For Custodians."

My mouth closed with a snap. Oh. So, this was where they hid. It was their sanctuary. I should've known. I shouldn't have asked. I needed to pay better attention if I wanted to avoid making mistakes like this.

"I see." The discomfort was like a heavy blanket I'd pulled over my head. Like an idiot.

It didn't seem to matter too much. He brushed off my clumsiness like it was nothing. Maybe he was used to it.

"How are you feeling?"

Although the hood was pulled low and I couldn't see his face in the shadow of it, I heard concern in his voice.

And it was funny, since I hadn't noticed how weak I felt until then. "Tired," I admitted.

"Me, too." Jonah even looked a little more pale than usual. His shoulders slumped.

Steward nodded. "You've been through a lot."

"Between fighting the Enforcers and coursing here, yeah. It's catching up to us." Jonah looked at me with concern written all over his face. "I'm sure it's affecting you more than me."

"Why me more than you?" I asked.

"Because I'm stronger than you."

"Says you. Remember, I have skills you don't." I heard the weakness in my voice, and I hated it and the fatigue that was setting in, draining me.

He only nodded. "We need to feed," he said. "That's the only answer. It'll restore our strength."

We both looked at Steward. He shook his head. "We have no blood here—there's no reason for us to store it."

My heart sank. Of course. They weren't vampires, so there was no reason to store the synthetic blood produced for creatures like us.

"Is there any way for us to get it?" Jonah asked.

Another shake of his head. "We couldn't run the risk of having a delivery sent here. I'm sorry."

"And feeding on others is against the law of the League of Vampires," Jonah murmured to himself.

Everybody knew that. The synthetic blood was produced to remove the need to feed on other creatures, which was one of the conditions the humans created when they agreed to make peace with us. They couldn't have us killing them anymore.

"We could still feed on animals, couldn't we?" I looked from one of them to the other, hopeful.

"I don't think that would be advisable," Steward said in a grave tone. "I didn't want to have to share this with you, but there have been Enforcers spotted in the area."

I couldn't help but gasp, remembering the fight with the ones we'd come across earlier. "No."

Jonah's arm slid around my shoulders. "There's nothing to be afraid of. We're safe here."

"You are," Steward assured me. "They could look every minute of every day for the next year and never see it—not just because it's hidden, either."

"What do you mean?"

"It's a matter of what humans are willing to see. If we're unwilling to see something, it can be right in front of our face but we'll be blind to it. They could stumble over the bridge leading to us and blame it on a rock or branch in their path. You might be surprised at the number of excuses a human is willing to make to cover up their ignorance. But they can't be blamed for it." Steward's shoulders moved up and down as he shrugged.

That was a relief. But it didn't help solve our problem. I was feeling weaker by the minute and wanted nothing more than to lie down and rest. That wouldn't help, at least not for a long time. I'd have to spend days resting to get my strength back, when blood—even synthetic blood—would restore me much sooner.

"There's one solution we haven't touched on," Steward pointed out.

I had no idea what he was talking about, but Jonah clearly did. His head snapped around to look at Steward.

"No," Jonah said. "I'm sorry, but no. You know it isn't personal."

"I understand," Steward replied in a controlled tone.

"I've tried it before and it didn't go well for me," Jonah continued, practically stammering in his discomfort.

"I have no idea what's going on right now," I admitted. "What's happening?"

Jonah turned to me, concern all over his face. "It might not be the same for you," he mused, one eyebrow raised.

"That's great, but I have no idea what we're actually talking about, and if I had the strength, I would scream at both of you for being so cryptic. So please, please, somebody clue me in."

From the look on Jonah's face, he was almost pained when he opened his mouth.

"He's suggesting you feed on him," Jonah clarified.

"On you?" I looked at Steward, eyes wide again. Would there be any end to the surprises this day? "Is that advisable?"

"I'm suggesting you both do it," Steward corrected. "I realize it's a shock after spending much of your existence feeding on synthetic blood, but it's better than suffering through the weakness you're feeling now. Especially since there's no telling how long it will take you to recover."

I could tell from his expression Jonah was fighting with himself. I wondered what the problem was with feeding from Steward, especially since it seemed like the only logical solution. Why was he so hesitant? I trusted Jonah's judgement, so the fact he was so reluctant didn't give me much confidence.

"All right," he sighed. "I guess we have to." He took my hand. "It'll be all right."

That didn't make me feel much better.

4

ANISSA

"Let's go somewhere you can be more comfortable once the feeding has commenced." Steward's face was expressionless, not judging.

It all seemed so formal, and the strangeness of the situation plus my growing weakness gave the impression everything was happening around me without my having any say in it.

Because, really, I didn't. I had no say. Decisions were being made for me and that was the way it had to be. By the time we reached the room Steward had picked out for us, Jonah was nearly carrying me. My head felt so heavy.

I couldn't help but remember Sara's weakness when we fled the mansion—she'd been so brave and strong, running as she had when she felt the way I did. In fact, she'd probably felt worse. My poor sister. Would I ever see her again?

I scanned the room. It was small, with a very welcome fire-place in which a very welcome fire blazed. There was a large sofa against one wall, piled high with cushions. I could almost forget I was in a cave, but the lack of windows reminded me.

Steward sat on the sofa then motioned for Jonah to place me beside him. Only I would have noticed the hesitation as Jonah paused for the slightest of moments before moving toward Steward, his arm around my waist. What was holding him back? Why was he so concerned? If I'd had more strength, I would have asked.

What had Jonah gotten me into? What could I expect?

"She's fading fast," Jonah said, but his voice sounded far away.

Was I dreaming? No, I was still awake. I could feel the heat from the fire on my skin—the little bit of skin still exposed, thanks to the bundling up I'd had to do. I could feel the cushions behind my back, too. And I'd never felt such deep, chest-clenching discomfort during a dream, either. Fear, yes, but not discomfort.

"We shouldn't waste time, then." Steward faced me and took hold of his hood.

I held my breath—what would I see? I swallowed back revulsion, although I had no reason to feel revolted. I hadn't seen anything yet, and I didn't know if there was any reason to feel revulsion in the first place. I couldn't offend him, either. He was allowing me to feed from him. That was no small thing.

When he slid it back, revealing himself, I marveled at the starkness and beauty. Steward's dark skin gleamed in the firelight —flawless, unblemished. His head was bald, as smooth as the rest of his face.

His eyes, however, disquieted me. They were amber colored, and, even in the dim light, they gleamed. They reminded me of the fire burning beside us.

Who was he? What sort of creature had eyes like his? He wasn't human, that was for sure. He wasn't a vampire. He wasn't fae. He reminded me of all I didn't know about the world, and that wasn't reassuring.

He tilted his head to the side, away from me, then ran a long finger down the side of his throat. "Here," he said in that deep voice of his. "This is the place."

I had no idea what I was doing, but I remembered the way Malory had fed from me. "Can I use your wrist, instead? It seems so intimate, using your neck."

He nodded, smiling a little. "You're right. Here." He held up his wrist, inside up. I looked down and noted the way the veins pulsed. I could see them so clearly. There was blood in them, pumping, waiting for me. For the first time in longer than I could remember, my instincts kicked in. I wanted his blood. I was hungry. It was the only thing that would help me. All I had to do was give in and take what was right there.

I closed my fingers around Steward's wrist, the sight of his pulsing veins hypnotic, pushing away all doubt. My fangs lengthened without my consciously choosing to make them do so. Centuries of evolution took over, as I closed my eyes and sank my teeth into his flesh.

He gasped, but he sounded just as far away as Jonah had been. Farther. Nothing else mattered but getting blood. Real, fresh blood. I groaned as I began to drink, my head swimming, my heart racing, every nerve in my body humming as I tasted the blood of a living creature.

No wonder so many vampires had risked so much for the taste of real blood. It wasn't only survival. It was intoxication, the feeling of flying although I knew I was sitting still. I was invincible. I could do anything, be anything, and crush anyone who stood in my way.

But, after my first gulp, things started happening.

Strange things.

Images flashed before my eyes. Images that weren't my memories. How could they be? I hadn't been in ancient Rome, had I? Of course not, I was far, far too young. And it wasn't a memory from a movie, or something I'd made up in my head after reading a book or a play.

No.

It was Steward's memories.

He was surrounded by others like him, tall, dark-skinned men-who-weren't-men, whose eyes gleamed the way his did. They were at the Colosseum, watching gladiators fight to the death. The stony expressions of the other Custodians didn't reveal much, but I felt how displeased they were. Yet they had no choice but to attend Caesar's events or else risk his animosity.

How did I know that? Because I was in Steward's head. Or his thoughts. I knew he was just as unhappy as they were, even as thousands of Romans screamed in delight all around them.

That memory faded. There was another, and this was of a fire. A fire unlike anything I'd ever seen—not the vampire Great Fire, either.

It was Rome. Rome was burning. And I watched it through Steward's eyes, standing in the doorway of a temple high on a hill with the rest of the Custodians. They'd known it would happen. They'd had the luxury of standing apart from the heart of the crumbling civilization, and they'd known it didn't have long to last if it continued on its course. But none of the ruling class wanted to hear the warnings Steward and the other Custodians had tried to give. So, they'd stood back and watched things fall into place, helpless to stop it. I could smell burning, could hear screams of terror and pain.

That image faded, too. I was no longer dressed in a robe. I was in a suit of armor, astride a horse. We galloped along open fields, little stone huts dotting the landscape. I smelled manure and fresh grass and heard hoofbeats all around me. I wasn't alone. There were dozens of others dressed like me, all of us on our way somewhere. And we were knights, carrying swords and shields. I knew enough about medieval history to understand what I was remembering. There were men working in the fields, women feeding chickens and tending gardens. And in the distance, looming larger with every step my horse took, was a castle. We were on our way to see the king. Which one? I didn't know. The memory wasn't clear or strong enough. I only had the impression of news we had to share with him.

Then, just as quickly, another memory swept over me. A much more modern one—the men and women around me wore jeans, skirts, sweaters. They stood in a large room, looking to each other for answers. I had the impression I was in the middle of a secret meeting. Then, I saw why.

A battle. Blood—so much blood. Humans using human weapons against those of my kind. Stakes and silver blades and silver shackles. Vampires tearing the throats from humans, leaving them dead in moments. Heaps of bodies everywhere, piled high.

And then, a new scene.

I watched as someone threw a lit torch into an open door. I couldn't see who did it, as it was dark all around me, but I did see the blaze that resulted. It grew and grew, higher and stronger, and it didn't take long for me to realize what I was watching.

The Great Fire.

I was seeing it set.

I was watching the Great Fire start.

The immensity of this struck me, but I didn't have the time to dwell on it as images rushed past in a blur. I couldn't make sense of them. So much fire, smoke, screaming. The smell of charred flesh was enough to turn my stomach.

My mother. I saw my mother fleeing the fighting around the outer rim of the fire—the flames hadn't quite spread there yet, and Mom ran alongside Sara's father. I wanted to scream to her, to get her to stop, to see me. But she wouldn't have seen me. She would've seen Steward. So, Steward knew her? Why else would I be seeing that very memory?

Another memory.

I screamed and screamed inside my head, knowing I was only seeing a memory but unable to separate myself from what I saw. It had happened so long ago, so very long ago, and yet it felt immediate.

Nothing could prepare me for the sight of my mother's corpse —charred, barely recognizable except for the heart-shaped locket around her neck. I knew that locket. How many times had I touched it?

Otherwise, the heap of burned flesh in front of me might as well have been charcoal. I felt hollow inside.

Another memory rushed in, obliterating the sight of my mother's body. I welcomed it. Anything would be better than seeing her like that.

Only Mom was in this memory, too. Standing in the center of a massive room. No, not a room. A cave. A cave... with walls lined with books...

My eyes flew open, and I jerked away from Steward's wrist. The entire sequence of visions had flown by in the span of seconds. The blink of an eye. I'd hardly slated my thirst, but that was the least of my concerns.

"My mother?" I asked, searching those amber eyes.

"What?" Jonah asked.

I hardly heard him.

"My mother was here?" I stared at Steward, willing him to answer me—of course, I already knew the answer, but I needed to know more.

He nodded. "And your brother."

5

ANISSA

I reeled back as though he'd slapped me. My face stung as though he had, too. All the breath left my body. Things started sliding around, out of focus.

"Anissa." Jonah took me by the shoulders and turned me to face him.

I could hardly see. I couldn't breathe. My brother.

I have a brother.

When I regained my senses, I let out a cross between a laugh and a sob. "I have a brother," I whispered. "It's impossible."

"I'll tell you everything you need to know, but, first, Jonah must feed. Whether or not he wants to."

I got up—I couldn't sit with Steward anymore, not after having seen his memories, not after having lived in his body for the briefest blink of an eye. I could see why Jonah wasn't a fan of the idea.

I waited in the corner while Jonah did what needed to be done. I couldn't watch when I knew what was happening to him.

Exactly what happened to me.

It was unnerving, seeing someone else's memories as clearly as my own. Going back to eras I had only ever read about. How old was Steward, that he was alive during ancient times?

I sensed rather than heard Jonah finishing, and turned to find Steward sliding his sleeves over his wrists again. Was it my imagination, or did his eyes burn a little less brightly than they had before we fed? It could've been a trick of the light.

"Tell me," I begged. "Please. I'll go crazy if you don't."

"Are you feeling well now?" he asked, almost like he hadn't heard me.

"Who cares about that?" My voice was savage with barely-controlled frustration.

He seemed unmoved by my passion. "I only want to be sure you can withstand what I'm about to tell you. I have to be sure you're strong enough."

I backed down a little. Of course, he only had in mind what was best for me. I had to stop flaring up like this if I wanted to get anywhere. "I'm sorry. Yes, I feel better. Much stronger."

"I think that's clear enough in your voice." Jonah stood there, leaning against the wall with his arms crossed. He looked much better already. Strong enough to be sarcastic, at any rate.

I sat cross-legged on the floor, near the fire. The warmth helped a lot. I didn't feel so lost when I didn't feel so cold. I knew I couldn't sit with Steward. I didn't want to run the risk of him touching me—my rational mind knew he couldn't show me his memories from a mere touch, but I didn't want to run any risks.

His eyes bored into me. "You saw, then."

"I saw quite a lot," I confirmed with a nod of my head. "From a very long time ago."

"So, you know how long my memory stretches back."

"I do. You've been alive for that long?"

For the first time, he smiled as he shook his head. "Those weren't all memories from my past. Not all of them exactly, but rather the collective memories of centuries of Custodians, all the way back to the beginning of time."

"You don't just keep books and scrolls," I whispered. "It's memories, too."

"Mine is a tremendous responsibility," he replied. "The same as any Custodian."

"Tell me about my mother, please. Everything you know."

He let out a great sigh that seemed to fill the little room. The flames flickered, making the shadows on the wall leap and dance. "Where should I start?"

"When was my mother here?" I blurted. "Please. Start there."

"Fifty years ago. After the Great Fire."

I slapped my hand over my mouth as I gasped. "But... that means..."

He nodded. "She lives."

She was alive! Hope burst in my chest, filling me with light even though I couldn't bring myself to believe what Steward had said.

"I saw her! How is that possible? I saw her body!"

And I would never forget it, either, her beautiful hair singed away, her creamy skin black and crisped.

"You saw what was left of her after the Great Fire, yes, but that wasn't the end of her life. She lived on."

"How? How, when she looked like that? She'd been burned beyond recognition—I only recognized her from the locket she wore."

"It was sheer will which brought your mother here," he explained. "She managed to crawl away from what was left after the flames died down. She must have crawled many miles, until she stumbled upon one of our hidden entrances. She slept many days at the mouth of the cave, unsure where she was. She only knew she was safe and away from the fire and the death that had surrounded her."

My poor mother. I wished I could've been there for her, but I'd been too young then. I couldn't imagine the pain she must've suffered dragging herself all those endless miles.

"Eventually, a young Custodian found her there." Steward shook his head. "He was reckless. He was curious about her, too. And I'm sure he felt for her—for all his faults, he was caring. So, he brought her into the Sanctuary and hid her for a long time. A very long time, indeed."

"How long?"

"It took years of her feeding from him to restore her to a semblance of her former self. In the end, it changed her."

"How?"

"It's not easy to explain. She was herself... But she was part of him, as well. A creature, even a powerful vampire, can only feed from another strong creature for so long before they begin to change. They begin exhibiting characteristics of that blood. Do you understand?"

"I do. And I guess after so many years, it was inevitable. She did heal, though? I mean, she didn't look horribly scarred or anything?" She'd been so beautiful. Her beauty was one of the most deep-seated impressions I still carried of her. Almost all I had left.

He nodded. "She did heal. No, she never was quite the same again, but she no longer looked burned."

"I see." I wondered how she'd felt about that. I wondered so many things.

"The Custodian who healed your mother was directly descended from the Archein," Steward explained. "The original shades."

"Oh, my gosh," I whispered.

"I, too, am descended from them," he added. "That's why it was so easy for you to access my memories when you drank my blood. The Archein blood is strong, full of the old memories."

"Are you related to the Custodian who saved my mother, then?"

"I am. He was my cousin." I noticed his use of past tense and decided not to ask about that. Had this cousin paid the ultimate price for saving my mother's life?

"You mentioned my brother. Who is my brother?"

"He's the son of your mother and my cousin."

I gasped. "They had a child?"

"I know my cousin fell very much in love with your mother over the many years it took to heal her. He was the only Custodian she was allowed to be in contact with, since she was in hiding throughout the time she healed. I suppose it was only natural they develop a deeper connection. And yes, they had a child. A boy."

She had another child. With another type of being. It was one thing to know she'd first been in love with my father, Gregor, a member of the fae. But this? This was something totally different. I didn't know what Custodians were, outside of the fact their blood was very old and strong. And my mother had borne a child with one of them?

"So, my brother is half-vampire, then, from my mother," I began, slowly, trying to feel my way through the situation. "And the other half is...?"

"You're asking what I am?"

"I guess so. Yes. I didn't want it to sound rude."

He let out what sounded like it wanted to be a chuckle. "I don't blame you for wanting to know."

"So?" My curiosity took over from politeness.

"I'm a shade."

"A shade?" I never would have guessed. "But... I thought shades were spirits. I mean, you're flesh and blood. Everything I learned about them said otherwise."

"Then you didn't learn everything," he explained. "A shade is not a spirit. Rather, we can house spirits. Many different types of spirits.'

"And my brother is half-shade, then?"

"Right. Half-vampire, half-shade."

"Wow." I wondered what he was like. Would I ever meet him? Would he want to meet me?

And where was my mother? She was never far from my thoughts. She was out there, somewhere, and she wanted me to think she was dead. Why? What happened to her? Why couldn't she show herself to me? It seemed like such a terrible waste of time we could've spent together. I understood she'd needed to heal, and she'd changed, but could she have changed so much just because she'd drank a shade's blood? Did that wipe me out of her memory? Did she forget she'd loved me?

"Where is my brother and my mother? Where are they?"

"I can't tell you. And I can't help you find them. I'm sorry." He stood.

"Why not?"

He exchanged a look with Jonah. I hated those wordless conversations. The sort of silent discussions grown-ups used when they didn't want a child to know what was really happening. Steward sighed. "Because it's already a risk to my life that I've brought you here."

"It is?" I gulped.

No wonder he hadn't wanted to tell me. I felt awful. I didn't want him to suffer because he'd saved us.

"And if the other Custodians find out I've given you blood, I'll face certain death. Our blood is highly valued."

"Why did you do it, then? Let us feed from you, I mean? If you knew it was certain death?"

He looked at Jonah again, whose eyes shifted to the floor. "Because Jonah saved my life. It's a blood debt. I owed him."

I stood, too. "And now what? Now that your debt has been paid?"

"Now, you'll stay here," he said. "You'll stay in hiding, of course. In my quarters. Meanwhile, I have duties to attend. Lessons are about to begin, and it's my night to lead the curricula."

"You teach lessons here?"

He nodded. "To the young shades. I have to be there—even if it wasn't my night, they'd miss me." He went to the door, which didn't take long seeing as how the room was so small. "Remember: do not leave my quarters for any reason."

"We were outside your quarters earlier, weren't we?"

I sensed his irritation at my questions, but it wasn't enough to make me back down.

"Yes, but we tend to sleep during the day. Now, the chance of discovery is much higher. Promise me you won't venture out."

"I promise," Jonah and I replied in unison.

With one more look at us, Steward left.

6

PHILIPPA

I was stunned. Yeah, that described me pretty well. Stunned. Speechless. Jonah had bolted. Just flat-out left our clan, left the league meeting, gave up. All for that half-breed, half-fae, half-vampire, white-haired girl. And now, I was going to be announced. I braced for the proclamation.

Lucian rose and took a few steps forward. "In light of these developments," he said in a booming voice, "it's clear Philippa Bourke is now acting head of the Bourke clan."

How the hell had this happened? I was still asking myself...

Jonah was gone. My brother, gone. He'd left. Never, ever did I think he would leave me like that. Sure, he was crazy about the little half-blood, but this? This was beyond insanity. It was reckless. It was stupid. And he'd just thrown me into a position I'd never imagined being in.

But who else could do it? Gage was gone. Nobody knew what he was thinking or when he would come back to his senses, the idiot. And Scott? He was younger than me, for one, and he was too busy making eyes at the little Carver girl. Little Miss Victim. She was crying softly then, most likely because her half-blood sister had run off and probably wouldn't be back. Not ever. I couldn't pretend I would miss her, but I would miss my brother. I would miss him a lot.

I stood there, willing myself not to shake. I wouldn't give any of them the satisfaction of watching me fall apart in front of them, even though that was exactly what I wanted to do. I wanted to break down and cry and ask the gods why this was happening to me. I'd never wanted to lead the clan. I didn't want the responsibility. Sure, I had advised my brother, but it was a lot easier to give advice when the outcome wouldn't be blamed on me if things went wrong.

I glanced around the table. Everybody was staring at me. All of the heads of all of the clans, including the Bourke clan. There was Marcus, sneering as always. This time, he looked as though he knew I would screw up. He was waiting for it. So, what if he didn't get his way and force my brother out of power? He thought he'd get what he wanted after I ruined the clan. He was so easy to read it was almost sad.

It was the expression on his face, that snide certainty, that stiffened my spine. I would have more than a few words for my brother when he got back from the delusion he was living in, but, for the time being, I was the head of the clan.

So be it.

I smiled as brilliantly as I could. "Thank you," I said, trying to sound gracious and strong. I had to. There was no choice.

I felt another pair of eyes on me, the only other pair I cared about.

At the end of the table, sitting closest to Lucian, was his clan. And in that group sat the vampire who focused so intently on me.

I could always feel when he watched me. I'd been able to feel it when we were together, before we were together, and in the years afterward. Some things never changed, did they? And Vance's gaze never changed. It felt hot, like a caress. It made my skin tingle and burn. I willed myself not to care too much. It wasn't the time. I had to focus on what really mattered, and seeing as how Vance was seeing a girl from Genevieve's clan, he didn't matter.

Still, I couldn't help but sneak a look at him from beneath my lashes.

There he was.

Watching me.

What was he thinking? How long had it been since I had been able to practically read his thoughts? Well, maybe not really read his thoughts, but I could almost always tell what was going on in his head. That was then, however. Far back in the past.

I couldn't bring those times back even if I wanted to—and considering how things had turned out, I didn't want to. It wasn't worth going through that pain again.

Did he believe in me? He always used to tell me he did. He used to tell me I was the smartest of all the Bourke kids, that I was the only born leader in the family. I didn't believe that—Jonah was a leader, for sure—but it was easy to be overlooked when you were the only girl in the family. Vance had always made me feel special. He'd made me believe in myself. He was why I had the courage to stand here in the first place, facing down all the disbelieving stares.

I couldn't let him know how much I still cared. I kept my eyes away from him as I sat back down. He'd moved on, hadn't he? It wasn't fair for him to sit there, watching me with those eyes of his, the way he used to when we were together. It wasn't fair. He couldn't be happy with somebody else and still keep me hanging on. The thought gave me strength and made it easier to regain control.

Scott, sitting at my right, squeezed my hand. I was surprised he knew what was happening around him, he was so stuck on Sara. I couldn't let her get to me, either. It was a fairly well-kept secret I didn't care for her or her half-blood sister, namely because I didn't advertise it much. I couldn't give her much of my headspace; she would only push me off track.

I had to present a good front—more than ever before. We'd

already lost Gage, and now Jonah. I had to show them we were strong. It was what my father would've wanted.

I sat blank-faced through the rest of the meeting, which I could tell the rest of the league were happy to get on with since my family had managed to cause so much commotion. My head reeled, my thoughts spun out of control. There were so many things to do, so much to take care of, and I was the one responsible for all of it. I tried to remember everything Jonah and I had ever talked over and knew it was pointless—I would never be able to remember all of it, and, besides, I would only overwhelm myself. I couldn't do that, either. I needed to take it slow. If I thought too far into the future, I'd only go crazy. One step at a time.

I was intensely aware of Marcus's presence, across from me. How many times had I said I wished I could get my hands on him? How many times had I wished I was head of the clan, so I could deal with him as he deserved?

All of a sudden, with the entire league looking to me for leadership of the clan and the rest of the clan depending on me, I understood why it wasn't so easy to lash out. It wouldn't be the smart move. I needed to outsmart Marcus, not try to defeat him by force. That was what he wanted, and I couldn't give him what he wanted. No, I needed to take advantage of the fact that he thought he was smarter than everybody else. He always managed to trip himself up due to that arrogance of his. I only had to sit back and wait for him to destroy himself.

I wished I could talk to Jonah about it. He would tell me what to do. How could he walk away like that? I thought I could count on him. I thought he was smarter, more reliable. Maybe Gage would've been the better leader all along. Gage wouldn't have let his feelings for some half-blood get in the way of what he needed to do. Duty would've come first, love or lust or whatever it was second. No, third, after family. Didn't family mean anything to Jonah anymore? I couldn't believe how much it hurt, thinking about what it took for him to leave.

I couldn't wait for the meeting to be over. I needed to be alone so I could process what happened, preferably somewhere I didn't have to sit up straight and put on my public face. I very much wanted to lie down in a dark room, alone, to think about all that had transpired.

When Lucian finally called the meeting to a close, I stood on shaky legs. The sounds of congratulations hung in the air as vampires from other clans wished me well. It wasn't sincere. I knew it. They didn't want me to fail, per se. They were only commenting on the excitement of it. They wanted to suck up a little. That was all. They'd sit back and wait for me to screw up. Well, I wouldn't screw it up.

"I need to get out of here," I whispered to Scott, and he nodded.

"We'll leave, then. There's a lot to deal with now."

He wasn't wrong. I hoped he was willing to forget about his little girlfriend for long enough to be a decent advisor to me. I needed the help. He was all I had. I would gladly throw that little Carver clan girl out on her skinny backside if it meant getting Scott's full attention.

"Let me freshen up fast." I, glanced around. "I need to splash my face and get myself together."

"Okay. We'll be by the door."

I waited for him and Sara to move to the door, making their way through the crowd, before ducking into the nearest restroom.

I was the only one in there, and I locked the door behind me to ensure I could be alone. Ugh, my eyes. They were wide, terrified. I needed to change the way I was thinking and fast if I expected to get past Marcus and make him believe I wasn't afraid to lead.

My skin appeared paler than normal, too, and my red hair stood out in stark contrast to it. I splashed cold water on my cheeks and leaned my hands on the edge of the sink while peering deep into my eyes.

"Get it together," I whispered. "You can do this. Don't let them see how you feel. You can't ever let them see how you feel."

That was one thing Jonah and I used to talk about a lot, not being able to let anybody else know what was happening inside his head. I finally understood that, really and truly.

When I was ready to leave, I unlocked and slowly opened the door. Then, I asked myself what I was doing. I needed to show a brave face. So, I flung the door open wearing a smile, head held high.

And I looked right into the eyes of Vance.

I glanced away instantly. He wouldn't get the better of me. He didn't even deserve the chance to try.

"Wait," he hissed, following me.

I pretended not to hear him.

Once I reached a little alcove just off the entry, he cornered me inside.

"What's with you?" His familiar smile was enough to curl my toes.

He had no idea how sexy he was. Oh, wait—yes, he did. He had a very strong idea. And that was one of the reasons why we'd broken up in the first place. His dark hair was pushed back off his forehead but still flopped forward a little, framing his chiseled features. His icy eyes gleamed beneath thick, dark brows that made them pop in contrast.

"What do you mean? I don't have time for this." I put my hands on my hips. "I mean it. Let me go."

"Not until you let me congratulate you on becoming head of your clan," he murmured. "I wanted to tell you how happy I am for you."

"That's a crock of bull, and we both know it. You're not happy for me."

"Sure, I am."

"You think this is all very funny. That's the truth."

"It's not the truth, and if you would ever give me a little credit, you'd know it. I'm genuinely glad for you. I think you'll make an excellent leader. I've always thought that, and you can't pretend I never told you so."

No, I couldn't. "Well, thank you. But like I said, I have to go. There are a million things to take care of."

"Like finding your brother?"

"Why are you hell-bent on making me want to hit you?" I scowled. "That's none of your business. Maybe if we were still together, it would be your business, but we're not, so it isn't. Sorry." I placed my hands on his chest with the intention of pushing him away from me.

He caught them under his hands and pulled me to him.

"We can change that, you know." He leaned in to kiss me.

I pulled back the instant our lips touched. Then I yanked my hands free.

"You're unreal, you know that? We broke up because you couldn't stay away from anything that looked at you more than once, and I finally wised up to that. I wouldn't stand it, so I told you to get lost. And I'm telling you to get lost again."

After I lit into him, he only smiled. How could he smile after I reminded him of the way he'd cheated on me? He'd broken my heart, the jerk.

"That was a long time ago—a very long time ago. I'm... Things are different."

"I'll believe that when I see it." I smirked.

"You can have the chance, if you want it. I'm moving to the city, and I'd like to see you when I'm settled in."

Oh, why did my breathing pick up speed when he said it? Why did I flush all over? Why did my body insist on betraying me in moments like this? I was afraid he knew what I was thinking, too.

"Yeah, well, you can keep wishing. In case you missed it in there, I have more important things to worry about now."

I pushed past him, and he let me go. I kept my gaze on the floor. I couldn't look around. I couldn't meet anybody's eyes. I needed to get out of here, and fast. When I was home, I could think.

"What's up with you?" Scott asked when I reached him.

"What do you mean? Aside from the obvious?"

"I mean, you look flustered."

"I can't imagine why. Don't worry, it's nothing." I couldn't push him away, even if I was in no mood to speak about my love life— or lack thereof. "We need to focus on finding Gage. We can't have him and Jonah gone."

Scott nodded. "I'll get to work on it as soon as we get home. Come on. It's been a long day."

Oh, he has no idea.

7

ANISSA

"Come on," Jonah said, taking my hand.

"Where?"

"I'll take you back to your room."

"My room?" I whispered my reply as he glanced both ways, up and down the hall, before leading me out of the small room and into the hall.

"Yeah, why?"

We spoke in hushed tones as we hurried back down the hall, in the direction of the rooms Steward had laid out for us. He had a lot of space in his quarters. I wondered if the other Custodians had room after room dedicated to their use. From the looks of it, most of the rooms were full of scrolls, texts, and the like.

"What am I going to do in my room?" There was nothing in there. Not even a window to peer out of.

"Rest. You need to rest."

"Rest? Who could rest right now?" I felt more keyed up than I'd ever felt in my life. My mother was alive. I had a half-brother out there somewhere and not a clue how to find him. It was easy for Jonah to tell me to rest. He had no idea how I felt.

"You should try." We reached my room, and Jonah stepped in after me before closing the door. Once we were inside, it was easy to breathe and relax. There was little chance of being detected in the hall, seeing as how we were in Steward's quarters, but still. The closed door helped me feel more secure.

"And you'll rest in your room?" I asked.

He grinned. "What do you think? I don't tell you to do things I wouldn't do myself."

"That wasn't exactly what I meant." I looked at the stone floor. So much like the walls and ceiling, though there was at least a small rug to give the room a homier atmosphere.

"You'll be fine." He put his hands on my shoulders, and I lifted my gaze to him.

"How is it possible?" I whispered.

"How's what possible?"

"Everything we've been through already. How's it possible? Didn't we just meet yesterday?"

He chuckled, and his grip tightened a little. "Maybe not yesterday. Maybe a little while before then."

"Okay. But you know what I mean."

He nodded. "I also know it feels like I've known you forever."

I had that funny, sweaty palm feeling again. "I'm not alone in that, then."

"No. You're not."

I couldn't decide if he was going to kiss me or not. For a heart-stopping moment, I thought he would.

Then, he released my shoulders. "I need some rest, too, I think."

I let him go, and only once I was alone did I start pacing back and forth in front of the fire. Every time I glanced at the flames, I remembered the fire from Steward's memory. I remembered the screams and the smell of burning flesh, both in Rome and during the Great Fire. Was this how my mother felt when she first started feeding from Steward's cousin? And she'd done it so many times, over so many years. It must have been overwhelming, the weight of all those memories. I hoped she'd been able to forget them over time, though I couldn't imagine forgetting what I'd seen and felt.

There was too much going on in my brain. Mother, brother, shades, memories. I'd seen the beginning of the Great Fire. I'd seen it start. Who'd started it was still a mystery, but I'd seen it with my own eyes. Well, not my eyes. Close enough. I felt so cold inside, like I'd never get warm again no matter how close I stood to the hearth.

And Jonah thought I should rest. He was crazy.

Nobody would ever know if I did a little exploring, as long as I stuck to Steward's quarters. He hadn't said I couldn't leave my room, had he? No. Only that I had to stay in his quarters. And I was doing that. I was also rationalizing. Even I could admit that.

It didn't stop me from opening my door and sneaking across the hall. The door to one of the rooms was ajar, so I slipped inside. What I saw in there just about knocked me off my feet. Scrolls. Stacked from floor to ceiling in all directions. What could they be? What knowledge of the world was stored in them? I almost didn't dare touch them. Almost.

There was a large, wooden stand in the center of the room—I guessed that was the spot where Steward would spread out the scrolls when examining them. A large candle-filled iron chandelier hung above the stand. There had to be some sort of enchantment on it, or else the chance of burning the whole room up would've been astronomical. And how terrible would that be, to lose all that knowledge?

I took one scroll at random from a small stack beside the stand and pulled at the linen ribbon holding it closed. Of course, it was written in some ancient language. I couldn't make heads or tails of it. How old could it be? If the Custodians had been spending time with the gladiators in ancient Rome, I could only imagine.

Then, I found something even older than Rome. The next text was written in hieroglyphics. Ancient Egypt! My mind boggled. Well, of course—the Archein were the first beings, as

Steward had explained. Where had they come from? Did they simply... appear one day? I didn't dare ask him at the time. I wasn't sure if I ever would. Could I handle the answer?

More and more. Latin, more hieroglyphics, ancient runes. Absolutely unreal. I was holding ancient information in my hands. How many hands had touched this over eons?

I was so busy imagining way back into antiquity I didn't notice the door opening until a presence stood behind me. I whirled around, prepared to flee if I had to.

"What are you doing here?" Jonah's eyes swept the room.

"Reading." I felt intensely guilty under his glare. He was disappointed with me. I hated that.

"Reading? Since when do you read Latin?"

"Oh, I know all sorts of things."

"You're smart. But you're not that smart." His hands found the sides of my face. I sighed softly—his touch was the best thing I'd ever felt, the best thing I'd ever imagined. Enough to make my breath come a little faster.

When he leaned closer, I realized he was going to kiss me. I wasn't wishing anymore or kidding myself. I closed my eyes and melted against him the instant our lips touched. It was like a spark leapt from him to me, or me to him. No matter where it came from, it created a sort of sizzling feeling that arced between us and spread all through me. I felt more alive. Everything was more real. I buried my fingers in his hair and held his face close as he kissed me. I wanted it to last forever.

But nothing lasted forever. Not even in our world.

"You need to get back to your room," he whispered, stroking my cheeks with his thumbs.

"Wow. What a romantic thing to say after kissing me." I was breathless, a little giddy.

He chuckled. "I'm serious. You can't be in here."

"But it's part of Steward's quarters, isn't it?"

"That doesn't mean somebody might not show up out of nowhere, especially in a room like this one. They might be looking for a scroll. Who knows? It's too much of a chance to take. We owe Steward that much."

I couldn't argue with that. "You're right." I didn't have to like it, but there was no defense against it. We went back to my room, where Jonah watched as I sat on the little bed Steward had made up for me.

"You'll stay?" he asked. I hated feeling like a child, like he thought he had to keep an eye on me.

"On one condition."

"Which is?" He raised an eyebrow.

"That I stay in your room. With you."

"Excuse me?"

"I don't mean that way." Though I wouldn't have been against it. "I mean I can't stand being alone right now. I can't. There's too much going on in my head. I need to be with somebody right now. Please. I'm alone in here, and my brain is racing out of control."

He paused for a moment then it was clear he saw how serious I was. "Okay. Come on."

We went to his room, which looked exactly like mine. "This is nice," I said.

"Uh, thanks. Not much like home, but safer."

"True." I walked the length of the room and back again, hands clasped in front of me. "I wish I could turn off what's happening in my head. Honestly. I really do."

"I know you do. But there's nothing you can find out right now. Is that what you were doing in there? Were you trying to find something?"

"It would've been nice if I could've."

"I think you're looking for a needle in a haystack."

"That's very helpful, Jonah. Thank you."

He snorted. "Sorry. I know it's easy for me to say."

"It is easy for you to say. You're absolutely right."

"But you know what? I can sort of identify with what you're feeling. I mean, I don't know what happened to my parents. They just... left. They went away." He was in a chair by the fire, his elbows on his thighs. He stared into the flames. "I don't know what happened to them. I don't know where they went. Are they dead? Alive? Why would they leave like that?"

"I feel the same way about my mother," I whispered, finally coming to a stop.

His words had calmed me a little because, yes, he knew how it felt. And talking about it made everything feel a little easier to deal with. "Why would she never come back? Why wouldn't she send word to me that she was alive? I mean, all these years... All these years and I thought she was dead. How could she have let me think that?"

"I don't know. And I didn't know her. But I guess she had a very good reason. I can't imagine being away from you and never telling you I was thinking about you. I can't imagine knowing I would never see you again." He looked at me, and when our eyes met I felt the same sizzling feeling I had when we kissed. "I can't imagine never being able to touch you again. So, there would have to be a very, very good reason for me to stay away from you."

He had no idea what he was doing to me. He didn't know how my heart threatened to burst when he looked at me that way and said words like that, or else he wouldn't do it. He wouldn't torture me this way—sweet, delicious torture. I wished we were anywhere else but here in this moment. I wished I could kiss him again and we could just be the two of us. We'd never had that chance.

"Why don't you try to get some rest? You need it, even with the blood."

"Okay."

I did feel calmer, actually. He had that effect on me. I stretched out on the bed, wishing he would join me but knowing it was better if he didn't. I closed my eyes, and, immediately, my body went into its resting state. My metabolism dropped as it always did when my body recharged.

I felt myself floating in a semi-conscious state, one ear trained for the sound of Steward's return. I had more questions for him.

Questions that couldn't wait much longer.

ANISSA

I didn't know how much time passed before I heard a commotion at the door. I sat up, looking at Jonah with wide eyes. His expression matched mine. Had we been discovered? One of the raised voices was Steward's. Who was the other?

At that moment, the door flew open so hard it slammed against the wall. I froze, terrified, sure we would be dragged out— or worse. I thought of the danger we'd put Steward in just by being there. Would they know we'd taken his blood, too?

There was a man standing there. No, not a man. Not exactly. He reminded me of Steward with his robe and those eyes. Eyes that gleamed even in hardly any light. Amber eyes. He was a shade, too.

But not only a shade. His skin was dark, but not as dark as Steward's. There was something else inside him, some other blood strain. There had to be. And his nose. His nose was like mine.

I sprang from the bed, facing him. It couldn't be. Steward would've told me. He would've.

Those amber eyes burned into me, and the shade whose nose looked like mine gave me a hard, cold look. He then gave Jonah

49

the same look, like he was furious and disgusted all at once. What would he do?

He turned and left, his footsteps pounding down the hall.

"Oh, no," I whispered, sure he would tell somebody we were there. "Who is he?" I asked Steward, who had moved into the doorway. "Is he going to tell we're here?"

Steward's voice was heavy when he replied. "He's your brother."

"My brother?"

Of course. It wasn't just the nose. It was a feeling I had as soon as I laid eyes on him. The same sort of connection I had to Sara was there, between us—different, but the same in many ways.

"Yes. His name is Allonic."

"I have to talk to him!" I dashed out into the hall, but there was no sign of him.

"Anissa, he won't want to talk to you," Steward said. "Please, trust me. You can't go looking for him."

"It's too dangerous," Jonah said, tugging on my arm. He'd followed me out.

I whirled to face Steward again. "How did he know we were here?"

"Allonic has skills. He must have sensed or felt you. I'm not sure."

"It doesn't matter. He knows." Jonah's jaw was set tight as he looked up at Steward. "What does this mean for you?"

"It means I have to find somewhere else for you to go."

"You don't think he'll keep us a secret?" But no! He had to. He was my brother. Didn't he feel the connection the way I'd felt it? How could he hand over his own sister?

"I can't say for sure. I want to believe he will, but I can't be certain." He looked downright flustered, and I felt sorry for him. He'd taken such a chance on us, too. "Wait here. I have to take care of things, do damage control if necessary. I'll be back as soon as I can—in the meantime, stay in your rooms and wait there.

Don't come out for anything." He hurried off, pulling the hood over his head as he did.

"We should listen to him," Jonah took my hand. "Stay in your room, and I'll stay in mine."

"All right." I had no intention of doing any such thing, but I had to at least make it look as though I did.

9

The second Jonah's door closed, I slipped back out into the hall. All of my old assassin's skills came back to me as I darted down the passageways, ducking in and out of the deep, dark shadows. It wasn't difficult to stay concealed since there was hardly any light brighter than a weak torch. I pressed myself against the cold walls any time I thought I heard footsteps or the swishing of robes.

I had to find Allonic.

Why had he run off like that? Was he angry to find me there? Why? Did he know who I was? Well, if he knew I was there, he probably had a good idea of who we were to each other. I held my breath as I heard footsteps from the other end of one passage, and, ducking into a shadowy alcove, I waited until the person passed.

There were so many hallways, a maze of passages both wide and narrow. I wondered if I'd ever find my way back to Steward's quarters. How large was the network of tunnels? How much land did it cover? I couldn't imagine how long it must've taken to carve it all out.

I heard voices, both male and female. There were female Custodians, too? Maybe my mother was one of them. Maybe she'd turned into one of them when she'd fed. Maybe that was what she'd changed into.

I pressed myself tight against the wall, feeling the cold rock beneath me. It sent a chill straight into my bones. I held my breath again as the voices grew closer. What would I do if they caught me? No. I couldn't let that happen. Why had I gone against Steward's orders? I could get him killed!

I glanced to my right, down a long, long passage. Torches lit the walls at even intervals, and I saw what appeared to be a female Custodian approaching. She was a little smaller than Steward but wore the same robe. The only thing that gave her away was the feminine walk and the curves that were hinted at beneath her robes.

She was coming closer with every step. Soon, she'd be right on me. Could she possibly miss me? I hoped so, but hoping wouldn't be good enough. My breathing quickened. I was sure she'd be able to hear it.

I couldn't take the chance. I had to course to get away from her. Although I still wasn't up to full strength after feeding from Steward, there was no choice. I turned and felt the mental *click* I was so used to, like my brain was switching to a higher state. My body became freer, and I started to let go.

Except, I couldn't course. I hardly moved. It was like I was trying to run through quicksand, like something was pulling at me. I'd had dreams similar to this before, where I tried to run or react quickly to something—usually it had to do with Sara and trying to protect her—but I couldn't, no matter how hard I tried. Those were always the worst dreams. I never thought it would happen in reality.

But there I was, struggling to move. I was sure the Custodian had seen me by then. There was no way she could miss me. Sure enough, I heard what sounded like snickering behind me.

"You can keep trying, little one. Exhaust yourself. It will make my job that much easier." Her voice was like a female version of

Steward's, slightly higher-pitched. And colder. Much, much colder.

She hated me.

I could feel it.

"What's... happening?" I whispered, still fighting against the pull she was clearly exerting over me. That was the only explanation.

The Custodian laughed. "Did you really think you'd be able to perform your little coursing trick here, little one? Did you think we wouldn't have layer upon layer of enchantment in place?" She was beside me, then, moving slowly to keep pace with me.

I turned my head slightly to get a better look at her, but her robes concealed her.

"We protect ourselves against that very thing—well, that and many other forms of magic which can be found in our world. We can't have ourselves being detected, now, can we?"

I studied her with narrowed eyes.

"You might as well give up." She walked around until she was in front of me.

I did exactly as she said, though I didn't want to. I didn't mean to stop. Why did I stop? What was she doing to me?

She lowered her hood, and I saw she had the same deep, dark skin as Steward's. Her eyes burned the same, too. She was beautiful in a cold, almost frightening way. It might have been the way she stared at me, like she was trying to get into my brain.

A tingling sensation began in my toes. I glanced down in surprise.

"No," she said, her voice sharp. "Look at me. Into my eyes."

I didn't want to. It was the last thing I wanted to do. It was terrifying, how much I didn't want to gaze into her eyes. Still, I raised my eyes to hers.

"That's right," she whispered. "Just look at me."

So, I did. I let her stare deep into my eyes and delve into my mind. I actually felt her digging in. And the tingling started to intensify. It deepened and grew. It began spreading all through my body, until my body wasn't my own anymore. I realized I had no control over myself—I told myself to move my arm, my leg, but nothing worked the way it should have.

Something wrapped itself around my senses. My eyes, my ears, my very thoughts. I wasn't me anymore. I was someone else—no, something else. The tingling stopped, replaced by numbness. Complete numbness.

I opened my mouth, ready to scream, to curse her. Nothing came out. I strained until my eyes bulged, but there wasn't a sound. All I could do was think, and my mind screamed. It screamed that I was trapped, that there was nothing I could do, that I was in bigger trouble than I'd ever been in.

The satisfaction in her eyes told me the Custodian knew I was under her control.

"Come with me." She turned and beckoned me to follow.

I had no choice but to do what she wanted. My arms and legs moved without my controlling them. I wanted to stop. I couldn't stop. I didn't know where she was taking me, but I had no choice. I had to go there. I moved like I was in a dream, like my conscious decisions meant nothing.

We walked for a short while then took a right turn and continued along a narrow passage with water dripping down the walls on both sides. She could've been leading me off a cliff and there would have been nothing I could do about it.

We reached the end of the passage, where a small door led to a small room. We were far from everything else. How often did other Custodians come to this area? My gaze darted around the room since I couldn't turn my head to look, still under the control of another. No scrolls, no books. Wonderful—the odds of somebody dropping by were slim, then. Of course, it wasn't as if I was waiting for another of the Custodians to save me.

But Jonah. How would Jonah ever find me? Why hadn't I listened to him?

"So, let's find out a little more about you."

Still under her control, I closed my eyes as the tall, dark figure drew closer to me.

"It's all right," she whispered.

I felt her rooting around in my mind, into my thoughts and memories, leaving me exposed and embarrassed. I wanted to push her out. I wanted to fight her. I couldn't. She was much too strong for me. Was this what shades did? Invade the minds of others?

She gasped and took a step back. She was awed by something. Me?

"You're part fae," she whispered.

Oh, no.

I'd heard that sort of excitement in a voice before when the subject of my mixed blood came up.

"Do you know how special that makes you?" she went on, circling me. "Do you know how valuable you are? Not only to me, but to so many others and for so many reasons? Oh, thank you for crossing my path. You're going to make me very powerful when I sell you."

Sell me? Not my blood, but me? To whom? To do what? What could anybody want with me? My flesh grew ran cold. Every conscious thought pointed toward fleeing, but there was no way to get my body to cooperate. Sweat trickled down the back of my neck even in the cold, dank room.

The door opened. My gaze cut in that direction. Jonah? Steward? No. Other Custodians. Other shades. So many of them. And all of them looked at me with contempt in their eyes.

"Who says you get to take her?" one of them asked my captor. A male. He reminded me of Steward, only there was no gentleness in his voice. I didn't realize Steward had a gentle voice until I heard one of his brethren speak.

"Yes. Just because you saw her first doesn't mean you get to take her for your own. We all know about her. We should get to split the proceeds."

"Split them?" My captor laughed icily. "It doesn't work that way, and you know it. I found her, I captured her, she's mine.

That's the way of the world. Find somebody special of your own and you'll get to keep the proceeds once she's sold."

Three or four different Custodians—shades, I needed to start thinking of them as shades and consider what they could do to me—circled around me. I heard them chuckling and whispering to each other. They thought it was funny I was under the control of one of them. Like I was a toy or an exhibit or something to amuse them.

"Make her slap herself," one of them suggested. The shade who controlled me smiled, and the next thing I knew, my right hand drew back and crashed into the side of my face. Pain exploded in a hundred directions from that one central point. Tears stung my eyes, both from pain and humiliation.

"Again!" Another one pushed the others aside and stood in front of me. "I want to see it again. I want to see the look on her face when she does it."

This time, it was my left hand. I slapped myself so hard my head snapped around. I willed myself not to let the pain show. I wouldn't give them the satisfaction if I could help it. Still, a single tear escaped and rolled down my cheek. Laughter filled the room, even over the sounds of bickering over who would get me for their own. Jonah had never seemed farther away than he did in this moment.

❧ 10 ❧

PHILIPPA

We walked out of the cathedral and into the moonlit night. The air was cool on my skin, which was a good thing. I needed to clear my head. Dozens and dozens of other vampires were walking around here and there, getting ready to course back to their home territory.

I couldn't help but notice Marcus and his band of vampires hanging back, watching everybody with distrustful eyes. That was their way. They wanted everybody to think they knew more than they did. Though they didn't think at all, the idiots. I doubted they had a full set of brain cells among them.

"Come on," Scott said again, taking my hand. In his other hand was Sara's hand, and I wanted more than anything to pull them apart.

Instead of letting my temper flare, I leaned over to him. "Don't you think you should cool it in public with her? Marcus is watching, you know."

"Let him watch. He wouldn't dare do anything to her while I'm here, not to mention most of the other clans, too."

"I know, but I think it would be best not to stir things up."

"Your first decree as leader of the clan?" he asked.

He was only joking, his usual way, but I was in no mood. I cut him a deadly glare that shut his mouth pretty quickly.

His gaze shifted from mine, and, seconds later, he dropped Sara's hand. They exchanged a meaningful look, and she nodded.

Well. She had more sense than her sister, anyway.

"Hey, Philippa!"

I glanced to my left, and my heart sank as Sledge walked over to me, his brow creased as he frowned.

"Where've you been?" I hoped to change the subject from what I knew he was going to say. If I took control before he had the chance, I might be able to steer things away.

No such luck. He might have been strong and loyal, one of Jonah's most valued and trusted guys, but he was as stubborn as an ox and about twice as quick on the uptake.

His focus moved behind me, to where Vance was walking—I could feel his eyes on me, as always.

"What's he doing with you?" Sledge asked, almost growling.

"What are you talking about?" I asked.

"I thought it was over between the two of you."

"It is," I said, glaring at him. "And could we please not talk about this right now? I mean, this isn't the time or the place." I looked around, reminding him we were hardly alone.

His loud, booming voice had attracted attention—and not the kind of attention I wanted. Like things could get any worse. I did what I could to keep from rolling my eyes.

"It is?" He stepped closer. The thumb he touched to my bottom lip was a total surprise—I didn't think fast enough to move out of his way.

"Why's your lip gloss smudged, then?" he asked.

I slapped his hand away. I didn't care anymore who saw or heard me. If anything, they would find out then and there I wasn't somebody to mess around with. "Don't you dare touch me like that without asking if I want to be touched," I warned him. "Besides, my lip gloss wasn't smudged until you touched it." Damn Vance. I could've torn his throat out.

"Oh, really?" He scrutinized my throat. "Why's your pulse racing?"

And didn't he go and put a finger against my neck, feeling my pulse? Though I told him not to touch me?

"Who do you think you are? A detective? Are you going to join the humans on their police force?" I glanced around again before saying another word. He needed to be set straight. "Listen, Sledge. Just because we had a couple of dates doesn't make you my husband. You don't get to interrogate me. And don't ever touch me without permission. I mean that. I have a real problem with it." I backed away and took Scott's arm.

After taking a few seconds to compose myself and let my adrenaline settle in, I waved a few of the others from our clan over to me, including Sledge. I hoped he could forget about his personal nonsense long enough to take care of what really mattered.

"We need to get to the building where Gage and his faction have been hiding out. Scott and I have been there before, so we know where it is."

Scott gave them the address.

I continued, "I can't have both Jason and Gage away at once. We can't. We have to put up a united front right now."

Moments later, we were coursing back to New York. There were six of us in total, including Sara. I wasn't sure she would be any help—in fact, she was a liability, since I couldn't be sure Scott wouldn't be too focused on her to take care of himself if we got into a fight. I wished more than ever she wasn't here.

The entire way back, I couldn't get my thoughts straightened out. Why did things like the blowup with Sledge have to happen when everything was falling apart around me? I didn't have the time or the bandwidth to think about Vance or Sledge.

And wasn't there anyone I could unload Sara on? I couldn't have her around. She would hold Scott back. I was sure of it. Of course, he didn't want to hear that. Nobody who thought they were in love wanted to hear the truth. How many times had Jonah warned me about Vance? But I'd gotten myself involved with him, hadn't I? I didn't want to listen to reason back then any more than Scott would now.

We slowed down once we reached the Bronx and the old building which Gage and his band of traitors were using as their headquarters. I recognized it from the first night we visited. Would he be there? He had to be. He'd have gathered his little group together for strength after the league meeting, for fear he'd been brought up somehow. He hadn't, but that might only have been because Jonah caused a bigger drama than his.

"Are you sure we should ambush them like this?" Scott asked.

"It's not like you to back down at the last second," I whispered. "Is there something I should know?"

"No. And I'm not backing down." But he sounded awfully defensive.

"What is it? Are you worried about her?" I didn't bother to try to hide the contempt in my voice. She was taking everything from me, everything I thought I could count on. She and her sister.

"Maybe I am a little," he admitted. "I don't want her getting caught up in this."

"In case you forgot," I hissed, "they're the reason we're in this mess with Gage to begin with, so maybe you'd better not worry about her too much right now. She's the one who got us caught up in something—her and her sister."

"All right. Point taken."

"Just don't tell me I need to feel sorry for her, all right? Because I don't. We're sacrificing so much, thanks to them."

"I get it. I told you I get it, and I get it. You don't need to keep rubbing it in like this."

"I'm not trying to rub it in." I sighed, already beyond frustrated, and we hadn't faced one solid day under my leadership. "I'm only reminding you we're your clan. Not her. And from what I've heard of her, she's tougher than she looks." I wasn't simply saying that, though. I meant it. I wasn't sure I could withstand the torture she'd been through and have the strength to run away from whatever she'd run from.

"You're right. I sort of feel like she's my responsibility."

"We're your responsibility. Your family."

"I know. I won't let her get in the way."

"Good. Don't." I waved the others over to us, and we continued to walk to the entrance. I looked around, all senses on high alert.

"Am I the only one who thinks there's something strange about this?" I muttered as we picked our way over broken concrete. The heels of my boots got caught in the cracks, and I cursed myself for choosing fashion over practicality.

"What do you mean?" Sledge asked. I wondered if he was over it yet and figured he probably wasn't.

"I mean the last time we were here, somebody called out the windows the second they caught sight of us. They made sure we knew they didn't want us here."

"You're right." Scott slowed to a stop. "Nobody's looking out. Nobody's warning."

"Nobody's there," Sara whispered.

I smelled blood. "No. Somebody's there." We must have all smelled it at the same time, since we all cocked our heads in the direction of the upper floors.

"Oh, you've got to be kidding me." I took off at a run with the others behind me. It couldn't be. It just couldn't. I wouldn't believe it until I saw it for myself.

I flew up the stairs two at a time, not caring about being quiet anymore because I had the feeling everybody who'd been here was dead. Which meant my brother. Would I find him here?

"Philippa! Wait up! You don't know if they've gone!"

Whoever *they* were.

Scott had a point, of course. I didn't know it would be safe to go up there alone, but there was no waiting when I was sure my brother was dead. I was certain we'd been tricked.

I reached the third floor, where the smell of blood was strongest. The rooms had been furnished since we'd been here, which was a lot of work for them to do in a short time. I wondered where they'd gotten the resources to put it all together and guessed Gage had something to do with that. He must have taken some of the family money to outfit his headquarters and make it more comfortable.

I got to a large room, probably once two rooms, but the wall separating them had long since been torn out. And that was where I found them.

At least two dozen dead vampires. Blood on the walls, the ceiling, pooled on the floor. Splashed on the furniture.

Scott came up behind me, and his curses were muffled under the sound of my blood rushing through my ears. I was sure I'd go crazy if I stared at it much longer, but I couldn't help myself. I had to remember it the next time I crossed paths with Marcus Carver.

"Look for him," I muttered, unable to do it myself. I couldn't bear the thought of finding him here, no matter what he'd done to us. I couldn't tell from a distance whether Gage was one of the bodies, since they all appeared alike when bathed in blood.

Sledge checked along with Pierson and Max, while Scott stood by my side.

"I don't think he's here." Sledge took my hand.

I noticed Sara standing off to the side, glancing around with wide eyes. Yes, she needed to be afraid. She needed to be scared for her life because I was roughly the blink of an eye away from slaughtering her. It was her clan—former clan, but whatever—who was responsible for what I was looking at. I had no doubt. Nobody could convince me otherwise.

"He's not here," Sledge announced.

I slumped a little, leaning against Scott. He wasn't here. My relief only lasted a moment. Fury replaced it.

"I want him dead!" I screamed.

I went to the next room, a random meeting room, and tore it apart. I threw a television through a window, swept a row of books from a shelf before tearing the shelf from the wall, shredded sofa cushions until the room was full of stuffing. It wasn't enough. I kicked a hole in the wall, then another.

"I want him! I want him dead! Gone! Finished!" My fangs were bared. I wanted blood.

"Philippa..."

I spun around to find Scott standing in the doorway.

"Don't tell me how to act right now," I warned him, my chest heaving up and down as I gasped for air. "I want Carver blood for this, and I want it now. They'll pay for this. And they'll die one by one until we find our brother."

And I didn't care if his little girlfriend approved or not.

❧ 11 ❧

JONAH

I couldn't stop worrying about her. Was that how I was destined to spend the rest of my existence? Worried over Anissa?

She was capable, but she was always getting herself into trouble. I had never known so much trouble all at once in my life.

And I had made the choice to go with her. I had walked away from my clan. I wouldn't choose differently if I had it to do over again, of course—I couldn't imagine existence without her. I just wished she would get a little better at staying out of trouble, was all.

I heard a noise at the door and sat up in bed, where I'd been trying to rest. The door opened, though it didn't burst open the way it had when Allonic came in.

Steward didn't enter the room, barely stuck his head in. "We have to go. Now. It's too dangerous for you here."

"What?" I jumped to my feet, ready to flee. "What happened?"

"Too much to explain now," he replied. "Come. We don't have a moment to lose."

"Let me get Anissa." I went to her room, next to mine, and opened the door... to find her gone.

"No," I whispered, as the world crashed in on me.

Why couldn't she obey the rules for once? Why was she always trying to take things on by herself? Didn't she ever learn?

"Come. We have to go. We can't stay here."

"No!" I said again, stronger this time. "I can't leave without her! You can't expect me to!"

"Jonah. It's too dangerous to stay. Come, now."

"I can't." I rooted myself to the floor. "I won't."

He sighed heavily, shoulders slumping. "You leave me no choice."

I knew what he meant as sure and as suddenly as if he'd struck me with a bolt of lightning.

"Don't do this," I warned.

"I have to."

I felt my toes tingling, the sensation spreading up from my feet to my calves, my knees, my thighs.

"I'm begging you," I said, but my voice wasn't as strong then.

I wasn't ordering or warning or threatening. I was pleading with him.

"Don't."

"You've made it impossible for me not to." Sadness filled his voice.

I opened my mouth to reply, but no sound came out as he took over my senses. My body went numb, like I'd been plunged into icy water. I had no choice but to follow him as he led me from the room.

It was a spirit, a spirit that had taken over me. Shades could host spirits as well as send them into others, turning us into hosts for those spirits. And we couldn't do anything to stop them. It wasn't fair for him to do that. My brain sizzled with fury as I followed him, helpless, to the scroll room where I'd kissed Anissa. What could he need from there? I didn't need a scroll. I needed Anissa. I needed answers.

I watched as he navigated the stacks and stacks of scrolls without disturbing a single one, even as his robe came within inches of brushing against them and toppling them all over. I followed, watching him closely. He worked his way to one of the room's back corners, where he moved a stack of ancient scrolls aside and reached into the small hole behind them. I couldn't see what he did, but whatever it was opened a door in the wall.

Dread filled me as we walked through the secret door and into a darker, colder set of tunnels separate from the rest of the Sanctuary. This couldn't be where Anissa was. He was leading me farther away from her, to the point where I doubted I would ever be able to get back. Where was she? Would she be safe there? Was she wondering why I hadn't come for her? I couldn't fail her, yet there was nothing I could do to fight Steward's control. The spirit he'd sent into my body compelled me to follow him blindly.

We walked on and on through a series of tunnels, ducking at times to avoid the low ceilings. I felt rocks scraping along my back, tearing into the thick fleece of the jacket Steward had provided me. Nonetheless, I couldn't flinch. I couldn't wince in surprise or discomfort. Nothing. I couldn't bend down lower to avoid being injured. It was like being in hell, I was sure. I couldn't imagine anything worse, not even starving.

Steward stopped abruptly in the center of what looked like a junction of sorts, with a handful of tunnels meeting at one point and going off in different directions.

I stared into the darkness and noticed a difference in the light, in the air near the spot where Steward had stopped. A sort of shimmering quality.

My eyes darted to Steward's face, looking for answers.

A portal? He was sending me through a portal?

Sure enough, my body continued moving, and I couldn't help but step through the circle of shimmering light and into the room on the other side. I was disoriented, foggy, totally unaware of where he'd sent me.

I heard him follow and, moments later, felt the grip of the spirit loosening. It was such sweet relief, I could have wept. I had control over myself again. I looked down at my fingers and flexed them, almost overjoyed at the way they obeyed my command. Before long I was totally my own.

I spun around to face him. "I thought you were my friend!" I roared.

I reminded myself I was head of the Bourke clan—or, rather, that I'd been born head of the clan. I had strength and power I'd chosen to leave dormant in the face of friendship. Betrayal had my blood boiling and friendship didn't mean as much.

"I am your friend."

"So, why would you do that to me? Do you know how that feels? Having to follow you around like some mindless thing under your control? Why? What did I do that you would treat me that way?"

"Believe me, it was safer," Steward assured me. "It had to be this way."

"Where are we? Where have you taken me? And where the hell is Anissa?" I looked around the dark, windowless room. "Where did that portal bring me?"

"I can't tell you."

"You'd better start talking," I snarled. "I appreciate everything you've done for me, Steward, but I'll still do what I have to do protect what's mine."

"Which is why I've placed you here," he replied. "I couldn't have you discovered while I'm distracted, searching for Anissa."

Hope bloomed inside me. "You'll still look for her?"

"Of course. I won't forget about her. I can't leave her there, either." He glanced behind him, to where the light still shimmered and flickered. "I can't waste any more time, Jonah. I'm sorry, but you'll have to stay here."

"Like hell I will!" I flung myself at him, but he put up a sort of shield around himself. I rebounded off it, hitting the wall behind me.

"I'll find her," he promised, as I shook my head to clear it. "I promise. I'll bring her to you, and we'll make a plan together. But it's safer that you stay here. I will come back."

"No! You can't leave me here like this! You can't."

"It's for the best. You'll see."

I jumped to my feet, ready to follow him, to do anything necessary to get to Anissa.

He held up one hand. "I haven't hurt you yet, Jonah, and I don't want to. Don't force me to."

It wasn't easy admitting to myself he was right. I was a powerful vampire, but my powers didn't mean much in the face of what he was capable of.

I watched, as helpless as ever, as he stepped back through the portal and left me on my own.

🦋 12 🦋

My face stung. Tears rolled down my cheeks. They made me pull my own hair, throw myself to the floor, and grovel.

I ached all over.

There were at least a dozen of the young shades standing around the room, throwing out commands for my captor to force me to perform, taunting me.

I could feel the presence of another inside me. Another being. A spirit. That was what shades did, wasn't it? They sent spirits into others. That was what the shade had done to me. I wished I knew her name. I knew nothing about any of the shades tormenting me.

I wanted to reach out to whatever was inside me. I wanted to ask what it was doing, how it was controlling me, if it could let up a little so the pain and shame could end. I needed it to end. I couldn't stand it anymore. I couldn't control my hands or the fresh tears flowing down my stinging cheeks and hitting the stone floor.

Please, talk to me, I thought, reaching out to the spiritwalker inside me. *Please, work with me, not against me. I can't take much more of this. Don't make me do this anymore.*

There was nothing but silence. Black, bleak silence. The hopelessness was worse than the pain, I decided. I was at their mercy, as I'd be at the mercy of whoever they sold me to.

Their voices mingled as they laughed and jeered and still argued over who should have ultimate control of me. I did what I could to tune them out, desperate for a little peace. I couldn't stand it much longer. They would drive me crazy.

"Enough!" Another voice cut through the cacophony. "Leave her alone."

I couldn't look up at him from where I was on the floor. I only knew it was a male, and not Steward. I knew Steward's voice well enough by then. It wasn't as deep as Steward's. Younger, too.

"But, we were—"

"I know what you were doing," he spat, shutting up the protestor. "Release her, Tasara. Now."

"You can't be serious," my captor, Tasara, said.

Tasara.

My captor's name was Tasara. I would never forget it, ever.

She would pay.

"You know me well enough to know I have no sense of humor. Let her go. Now."

And just like that, the tight hold over me loosened. I could control my head, my hands, my legs.

Except I was too weak and downtrodden to get up.

Instead, I closed around my core, drawing my knees to my chest and wrapping my arms around them. I couldn't stop shaking. I closed my eyes, willing myself to shut it all out. I couldn't bring myself to stand up to them and show them they hadn't broken me. Because they had come very close to doing just that.

"I want you out of here, now," the voice ordered. "And you know better than to talk about this to any of the others. Your punishment will be severe. No one is to know she's here. Is that understood?"

"But—"

"I mean it, Tasara. Now go. All of you."

I heard their robes shifting as they left and felt the resentment boiling in the shades Like a bunch of naughty kids who'd been caught. Who had discovered me? Probably the leader of the Custodians. Was he saving me for worse punishment?

"Get up."

He was talking to me. There was no one else in the room.

What he didn't know was I couldn't get up. I was terrified, not to mention heartsick.

"Anissa." The command in his voice and his knowledge of my name opened my eyes.

I looked up—slowly, inch by inch, taking in the robes and the dark skin that wasn't as dark as Steward's. The eyes. That nose.

"It's you." I unfolded myself, awe taking over for fear. I was too stunned by the presence of my brother to worry about how I felt anymore. "I don't believe it. You saved me."

"I didn't."

"You did. I never would have survived that without you. Thank you."

He glanced away as I stood. "I didn't do it for you," he muttered.

"Who, then?"

"For our mother." He looked at me again, but only briefly before his eyes shifted away from mine. "She wouldn't want to see her oldest child in that position."

I heard respect in his voice, maybe even love. I wondered about the two of them. How long had she lived here with him? How much did he know about her? And he knew about me— how? Had she told him he had sisters out in the world? Did he ever wonder about us?

"I have so many questions for you," I whispered.

"I'm sure you do, but now's not the time for them."

"When, then? I'm tired of being told now isn't the time. Wouldn't you want to know?"

"I've always wanted to know."

He met my eyes at last, and I saw pain in his

"But like I said, now's not the time. You aren't safe here. One day, I'll let you feed from me and you'll get your answers. For now, we have to leave."

"Leave? And go where?" And without Jonah? He knew about Jonah, of course. He'd seen him. I was afraid to mention his name for fear of how Allonic would react. He was saving me because I was his sister. That didn't mean he had to save Jonah. If I brought him up, my brother might abandon me.

"Out of here. I'll help you find safety elsewhere."

"But where? Out in the world? I don't know what time it is out there. I could burn in the sun if it's still day."

He nodded. "And it is. Most of us are settling in for sleep at this time, to avoid being awake when humans are most likely to be in the forest around us. There's still a lot of time before the sun sets. It'll have to wait until then." He turned away, like he was about to leave.

"Where are you going?" I hated the sound of panic in my voice but couldn't do much about it.

"I have to leave you here for now," he said, staring at me with those unnerving eyes of his. "I'll come back, and we'll get you out of here then. Just wait for me here."

"What happens if one of them comes back?" I couldn't keep from shivering a little at the thought.

I would never forget her. Tasara. Her taunts and jeers. The way they'd all made me hurt and degrade myself.

"They won't. They know they'd have to face me if they did, and none of them want to do that. Trust me." He didn't say another word, his robes trailing behind him as he left the room.

Wait for him here? Wait for one of them to come back for me, more like. I couldn't take the chance. I didn't know if I could trust him—I remembered the way he'd looked at me when he first discovered me in Steward's quarters. His expression had screamed hatred and resentment. What if Allonic was only saving me for himself? What if he had something worse in mind for me?

I didn't intend to hang around and find out.

I slowly counted to one hundred, until I was sure he was far away, before opening the door.

How could I find my way back? I dashed down the long, dark tunnel Tasara had led me down when I was under the control of her spiritwalker, then made a left since we'd made a right. Yes, I remembered. I'd made a left turn three doors down, so this time, I made a right when I was sure there was no one around to see me.

I was careful, staying close to the walls, freezing in place whenever I thought I heard voices or footsteps. It was all in my head—I was still shaken up by everything that had happened back in that room. I pushed it aside. I had to focus on finding Jonah.

Once I reached the towering room with the rows and rows of shelves, I knew I was on the right track. I ran down the hall Steward had led us through until I was back in his quarters. I could breathe here. I leaned against the wall outside the door to my room, eyes closed, chest rising and falling rapidly.

"Jonah?" I whispered, once I'd collected myself.

I opened the door to my room—empty, as I had expected it to be. I went to his room next.

"Jonah? Come on. We have to leave, right now. It isn't safe."

Only he wasn't there. His room was as empty as mine. Dread grew in my stomach. How long had I been gone? What could've happened to him? Anything, really. What they'd done to me might have been just the beginning. And to them, he wouldn't have been as valuable—he didn't have fae blood. They could have...

"Jonah?" I was desperate, my heart racing as I went from room to room. Each was empty except for books and scrolls and documents I no longer cared about. I only cared about finding him. Where could he be? I didn't see a trace of Steward, either. No. They wouldn't have left me here.

Maybe they did. Maybe they gave up, or maybe things got so dangerous for Jonah he had no choice but to leave. Maybe he was hanging around somewhere at the entrance to the cave, waiting for me to come out. I had to go. He'd be there. I was sure of it.

How had Steward brought us to his quarters? I closed my eyes and willed myself to look back. I replayed what I could in my mind, calling up the little landmarks I could remember. I had been so confused then and so afraid of where we might be going I hadn't paid the strict attention I could have. I cursed myself for not being more aware. I should've been.

I couldn't stop. That much was for sure. I kept going, through long, dark passageways.

I headed away from Steward's quarters until the cold wasn't so cold anymore, making rights and lefts as necessary, until there weren't any more doorways. It was all smooth wall, floor, ceiling.

I realized I was on the right track and started to run. I remembered the long passage he'd led us down when we first came to him. When I reached the end of that, I spied a glimmer of light at the end—mouth of the cave entrance. My heart soared.

"Jonah?" I called as I ran. He had to be here. He just had to. He'd make everything better. I wouldn't have to worry about anything anymore.

I didn't stop running until I was in the open, and immediately I recoiled away from the sun's burning rays.

"Jonah!" I cried, wanting him to know I was here looking for him. He had to be hidden somewhere. That was the only answer. He was hiding, protecting himself from the sun until I found him.

"Jonah, I'm here!" I covered my face with my arms, but it was no use. My bare hands began burning almost instantly, the back of my neck, too. I covered it with one arm, but that left part of my face exposed. I shrieked, spinning in circles, trying to find somewhere to hide until the sun went down again.

I was too weak and too scared to go back inside—what if somebody found me when I did? Yet I blistered more and more every second I was in the sun.

Images of my mother's charred body flashed across my mind. I heard the skin on the back of my neck sizzle.

There was only one thing to do. I began to dig, using my scorched hands. It was even greater agony, and it left my head and face exposed to the brutal rays. Although I worked blindingly fast, throwing dirt and leaves in all directions as I dug myself a hole to hide in, by the time I finished, my hands were a mass of raw blisters.

I scrambled into the hole, sobbing in pain as my scalp began to swell up the way my hands had. I pulled the leaves and dirt all around me as the skin of my face began burning and peeling.

Hurry, hurry, hurry.

I settled in once I was completely covered, one mass of gripping agony. Not even the slimmest ray of light pierced the shelter I had created for myself.

I closed my eyes, wondering what could possibly happen next as I prepared to rest and heal. I couldn't look for Jonah while the sun was up and while I was in this condition.

"Please, wait for me," I whispered, though I knew he couldn't hear me, before closing my eyes and allowing myself to go into a state of stasis for healing.

13

It was taking too long.

I opened my eyes, listening for the sounds of the forest. There were almost none—the sun must have set, the daytime animals inside for the night. Even the birds no longer twittered in the trees. The nocturnal ones were emerging from their dens and the shadows.

I was too weak after my experience with the shades, the spirit-walker, and the burning sun's rays. I had never fully recovered after feeding from Steward, either—the visions I'd seen had made me break off before I was finished. I couldn't heal fast enough when I was weak like this. The pain wasn't as strong as it had been—it was still there, but it had dulled to a slightly more reasonable ache. My hands weren't oozing as they had been when I first hid in the hole.

It would have to be enough. I couldn't wait days to find Jonah, and I couldn't risk leaving myself out in the open even if I was concealed in a hole.

I had to feed.

On what?

I focused my vampire hearing, but couldn't make out the sound of anything larger than a rat. There was nothing big enough

81

to bother feeding on, and I didn't particularly enjoy the idea of feeding on a rodent, anyway.

A footstep caught my attention.

Another.

Jonah, I wondered.

No. I would have known if it was him. I didn't know how, but I would. Maybe because his step was much lighter and more graceful than the heavy, plodding tread I heard to my left. Maybe twenty feet away, from the sound of it. A hunter? No. Not at night.

So, it wasn't someone hunting for animals. It was someone hunting vampires. An Enforcer.

Even in my weakened state, I could overtake him if I tried hard enough, and if I had the element of surprise on my side. All of my training came back to me. I could thank Marcus for that, at least. I knew how to be quiet, so quiet my prey had no idea I was anywhere near until they felt my thin blade slip into place.

It wouldn't be a blade this time. It would be my fangs. And I couldn't use the wrist—he could fight me off with the other hand if I did that. No, I had to latch onto the throat and wrap myself around him so there would be no chance of shaking me off. Did I have what it took? I needed to, or else it would mean waiting endless days to heal. And there was no synthetic blood for miles and miles.

I waited until the Enforcer was far enough away that his footsteps were barely audible before I rose from the ground. Luck was on my side for once, as clouds covered the moon and hid my rising.

The Enforcer was only thirty or forty feet away, on the edge of a clump of trees with his back to me. I could almost smell the blood pulsing through him, waiting to replenish me. I couldn't afford to linger—he might see me—so I ran to him and threw myself onto his back.

"What—"

That was all he managed to say before I pulled his head to one side and latched onto his neck at the spot where the artery pulsed beneath the skin. He had been carrying a crossbow but dropped it in surprise.

Not much of an Enforcer, obviously.

I closed my eyes and drank deep. I was breaking the league's laws, but I couldn't worry about that. It was a matter of survival. I wasn't feeding for the sake of feeding, out of convenience or anything like that. It was feed or die.

And no wonder they didn't want us to feed from humans.

It was like a drug hitting my system all at once. I took big, long gulps, filling my senses with sweet, tangy blood as I drank. The human's heart pumped rapidly in terror as the man fell to the ground, sending the blood in great gushes into my greedy mouth.

Yes, no wonder they didn't want us to feed from them. It made me feel invincible! I could do anything! I buzzed from head to toe, filled with an energy I'd never known.

The heart began to slow and, with it, the flow of blood.

I sucked, hard, trying to get all I could before I killed the human. I couldn't drink once he was dead—we couldn't drink from the dead, not ever.

It would kill us as surely as we killed them. I waited until the man was a heartbeat or two away from death before disengaging, and even then, I was reluctant to leave him there. He was still, deathly still.

And me?

I was on fire from the inside out, a fire I could get used to. Everything was sharper, clearer. I could hear everything. I could see everything. I was strong and fast and powerful. Nothing could stop me.

And I was healed, too. No more burns or blisters. Nothing but smooth skin.

I had to find Jonah. He was all that mattered. I shook my head to clear it of the almost-drugged state I was in and began searching. I was faster than ever thanks to the blood, and I listened intently as I covered the forest in hopes of finding some sign of him.

But first, I needed to try to hide the body. I hastily covered it with leaves and branches, not satisfied until I couldn't see it easily.

Now, to find Jonah.

I didn't hear any movement but my own and that of a few owls and bats. The moon's light cast a silvery glow over the trees, but it didn't help me find Jonah. My frustration grew. He had never left the Sanctuary, had he? He had to be in there somewhere, in the maze of tunnels and passageways. How could I ever find him? Was he still alive?

I hurried back to the hidden entrance, unsure of whether I should take the chance of going inside again. What was waiting for me in there? Jonah wouldn't leave me, would he? No. If he could, he would rescue me. I remembered the way he'd saved me before, at Mallory's. He'd just about charged into hell for me. I couldn't abandon him.

I entered.

The hair on the back of my neck stood straight up. There was someone nearby. I sensed him—or her—somewhere close to me. I couldn't tell if it was friend or foe. I froze for a second before spinning to find Steward behind me.

"You're here," I breathed, relief flooding me.

"So are you."

"Where's Jonah?" I looked around, sure they'd be together.

Steward's eyes blazed. "I had to move him to a safer location since your decision to go off on your own put us all in great jeopardy." He was angry, disappointed, frustrated with me.

It was clear if taking care of me hadn't been a favor to Jonah, Steward would've told me to get lost.

"I'm sorry."

"It doesn't matter now," he replied. "I'll take you to Jonah."

"Thank you." I had to see him. I'd almost been sure I never would again, especially if Tasara had her way and sold me off.

Who had she been intending to sell me to? Well, they'd have to be disappointed.

A tingling sensation began in my toes. I knew that feeling. I looked down, eyes wide with horror. "No. Don't do that!"

"I have to. There is no choice." Steward's voice was nearly hypnotic.

"I mean it! I don't want one of those things in my head, ever again! You can't!"

"This is the only way."

My legs went numb. My hands. My arms. I struggled and fought and writhed and nearly screamed before my voice was cut off, too. I wasn't alone in my body anymore.

Not this time.

I wouldn't let it happen. I struggled inside, determined to fight it off, unable to move but still able to think. Steward merely stared at me, and I didn't know if he was surprised or amused or both. He probably thought it was funny I imagined I could fight him. I would show him what I was capable of.

Only it wasn't that easy.

I found the spiritwalker just as I had found the other one.

Leave! I screamed, imagining myself closing a door to block it out of my thoughts forever.

"What do you think you're doing?" Steward asked, but his voice was far away.

I don't want you here! Go away! Get out of my head! I yelled at it in my mind.

I couldn't get through to it. I imagined it here, nesting in my brain, with its tendrils running all through me. Gripping my mind.

Let go of me! I ordered it, but it merely nestled in more snugly.

'You can fight the spiritwalker,' a voice said in my head.

I heard the voice as clearly as though it was right beside me. I couldn't turn my head to look around, of course, but my eyes swept the area I was in.

The light of the moon still shone, but I couldn't see anyone. I couldn't feel another presence, either. I could only hear the voice in my head.

I can't fight it! I replied to the voice. *I'm trying, but I can't!*

'*You can. You simply don't know how to work against it. A spirit-walker isn't swayed by false bravado.*'

It isn't false. I'm brave.

'*Sure, you are.*'

I heard sarcasm but chose to brush it aside.

How do I fight it, then? Please, help me. I can't do this again.

'*Use your inner sight. You can find it inside you if you use that power, and, once you've isolated it, you can battle and defeat it. I know you can. You have the power inside you. You only have to use it. Stop fighting blind and start fighting smart.*'

Use inner sight?

The voice didn't tell me how to use inner sight. I never had before.

Still, it was worth a shot. I concentrated all of my consciousness on finding the spiritwalker within me. As I did, something washed over me. I still couldn't move, but I didn't feel like a mindless, helpless shell anymore. I felt like I had the strength to do what I needed to do. If only I knew exactly what that was.

'*Draw a cloak around you,*' the voice said in my head, as if it were listening in on my thoughts.

Instead of being angry or feeling violated, I felt calm.

'*Once you do, you'll have the spiritwalker trapped. Then you can battle it—it won't be able to rely on the power of the shade to protect it if you isolate it that way.*'

I understood. I envisioned myself searching for the spiritwalker inside me. Where was it hiding? Not in my brain, as I had imagined, but in-between the brain and the subconscious.

There it was.

I pulled the cloak around myself, envisioning cutting the two of us off from everything around us. There was only blackness. Blackness, and the two of us.

A wraith stood before me, cloaked in long, tattered robes. It raised one bony arm and pointed at me. Did it think it was going to frighten me?

None of this is real, I told myself, not really. It only exists here, inside me. And I made the rules here.

It shuddered, but only for the briefest of moments before it lunged at me. I almost didn't have the chance to dart out of the way, but I was quick enough that it missed me. I had the upper hand. I only had to remind myself of that.

I threw myself at it, pushing it away. It was already off-balance after missing me, so the element of surprise was on my side, too. I wished I had my weapons with me—then realized I could, if I wanted to. I imagined my silver blade in my hand and there it was, shining against the blackness.

The wraith screamed horribly, but I withstood the ear-splitting sound as I threw myself against it again.

Get out! Get out of me! I screamed at it, pushing it away with all my might.

It knocked me back a step or two, but that wasn't enough to stop me. I was determined. I finally knew what I was fighting.

Go! Get out!

Its bony fingers wrapped around my wrists as it screamed again, white eyes blazing from beneath its hood. There was nothing in those eyes. Nothing at all. We were face to face, pushing against each other, battling for control.

I knew without being told not to stare into those eyes. It would be worse than death to look into the eyes of a wraith. I'd be lost forever.

Let go of me! I screamed at it in my mind and shoved harder, enough to knock the wraith back and make it release my wrists. I thrust my blade into its torso, where the heart would be—if it had a heart.

It screamed louder than ever, a horrible sound that threatened to tear my mind apart. I couldn't take it. I was sure it would drive me crazy if it didn't stop. I covered my ears, even though the sound was in my head and there was no way to block it out. The wraith died in agony, screaming and falling to the ground.

Then as it vanished.

Back in the physical world, I fell to my knees. I was exhausted, totally drained, and not sure what had happened.

"You killed it." Steward sounded stunned. "How did you do that?"

I breathed heavily, as drained as if I had coursed for hours. I couldn't make sense of what had happened, not a bit of it. Still, I felt victorious. I had won. How had I won? I still wasn't sure, but I had.

A crunching sound—like that of a twig or leaf—startled us both, and I jumped a little as Steward turned toward the noise. The next thing I knew, a branch swung around and hit Steward in the back of the head. I screamed softly, pressing myself against the wall, ready to run.

"You did well." Allonic stepped out of the shadows, dropping the branch as he did. "I knew you could do it.

"Wait... that was you? You were the voice in my head?"

"It was me."

"Why did you do it? Why did you help me?"

"Because I wanted to see if you could do what I knew you were capable of. And I wouldn't let him control you that way, especially when you begged him not to do it."

"Thank you. It was incredible. I didn't know I was capable of something like that."

"I did. As I knew you were going to run away the minute I left you alone."

He seemed to know me, after all, though we hadn't met before this. Maybe it ran in our blood.

I couldn't celebrate my victory any longer. I couldn't waste another minute. "I have to find Jonah."

Then, something else occurred to me.

"You just knocked out the one person who can tell me where he is!"

❧ 14 ❧

PHILIPPA

I looked over the heads of the vampires assembled in the lowest level—the basement—of the high-rise we called home. There were probably two hundred vampires, give or take a few. We were the only ones who knew of the elaborate tunnel system beneath our building.

The tunnels had been completed decades earlier. We'd needed a way to get around the city without being seen, and traveling underground had been the only way to go. It was perfect for what I had in mind.

I clapped my hands to get the attention of those in attendance. "Thank you for being here," I said, standing on top of a table at the head of the assembly room. It was so strange, being at the head of the meeting. I'd had to psyche myself up to build the courage to speak to so many of the clan at once.

What did they think about me standing here? Did they think it was a joke?

I definitely saw more than a few confused expressions, not to mention a few expressions of disbelief.

They must have heard what happened at the league meeting, of course, and they'd always known me to be the party girl of the family. That was my *thing*, wasn't it? I was never very interested in living by the rules of others, and I'd seen enough death and destruction—not to mention hearing the stories told by vampires much older than me about the destruction of the Great War—to take my existence very seriously. Talk about a turnaround. I couldn't wait to get my hands on Jonah.

But he wasn't my first priority. One of the new lessons I was learning about leadership: prioritizing. Gage was number one.

"Well, I guess you all know," I said, deciding I might as well address the elephant in the room. "Jonah left. He chose something that was important to him, and we have to support him in his decision." Oh, how I choked on the words. I didn't believe them for a second, but I needed to make the others believe them. We had to unite. "Lucian and the rest of the league decided I'd make the best choice for leader of the clan, and I have to agree with them."

There was a rumble of laughter throughout the group— friendly laughter, which was a good sign. They were on my side. Good. I needed them there.

"What you might not know is I've been Jonah's closest advisor for decades. I know almost as much about heading the clan as he did. He came to me with almost everything, so I'm well aware of our position in terms of relations with other clans. Which brings me to my next order of business, and the reason why I assembled you all here now."

I glanced down at Scott, who gave me a firm nod. I'd already practiced my speech on him a few times in the hours since I'd called the meeting.

He'd helped me make it more "relatable," as he called it. I needed to make them like me. I was never great with that—I could party it up with the best of them and get along with just about anybody, but that was all superficial, surface-level stuff. This was the real thing, and leading people was more of a challenge for me.

"As you've heard, Gage is missing."

The rumble of murmuring after that statement was a lot less

friendly than the laughter I'd just heard. I held up my hands to quiet them. "Listen. I know how you feel. I'll be honest with you —I think you deserve that much. I hated Gage when he left. I felt he'd betrayed me, and I'm not one to forgive a betrayal easily. So, I don't blame any of you for being angry with him. I don't blame you if you don't care what happens to him."

There was more rumbling.

I held my hands up to stop the noise.

"But!" I continued. "We have to remember something important, something that runs deeper than our feelings or opinions on Gage's decisions. He's our blood." I looked around the room, deliberately making eye contact with as many of them as I could. "We don't give up on blood. No matter what, we can't leave him in the hands of the Carver clan or any other clan. He's ours. If we want to deal with him, we'll do that in our own way—but it'll be up to us. It doesn't mean we abandon him. And I guarantee you, whoever kidnapped him is counting on us not coming for him because we've cut him off. We can't fall into that trap. We can't give them what they want."

A few heads nodded. Then more. Pretty soon, I knew I had the majority on my side.

"So, we go looking for him. We find him, and we bring him home because he belongs to us. Not to them." My voice shook with emotion. It was mostly rage, but a little might have been love. Because I still loved him. I thought he was an idiot for doing what he'd done, and I didn't know if I could ever trust him again, but I loved him.

"Yes!" I heard from the back of the room. A chorus of cheers erupted, and I was sure the echo would deafen me. But it was a good feeling. I could see why others enjoyed leading—at least, when those they led were on their side.

"Here's what we're going to do. We're going to spread out in groups of twenty-five, each group led by our senior clan members, and we're going to find out as much about the Carvers as we can. We know where they spend their time and have chosen spots through the city to surveil." I divided them up, and they shifted until they were in their groups.

"I'll be waiting to hear what you find. I know we'll be able to find out where they've hidden Gage. As soon as you hear anything —anything at all—get back here and inform me. I don't want any of you taking chances you don't need to take, either. Be careful out there. Let's bring Gage home."

They left in high spirits and spread out through the tunnels which went on for miles, covering the entire city. There had to be something out there. Some clue.

The hardest part would be waiting to hear.

I let out the breath as the room nearly emptied.

Scott gave me a thumbs-up, and I smiled in gratitude.

"I couldn't have done it without you," I reminded him.

"Sure you could have." He grinned. "You were the one up there calling everybody to action. I was halfway ready to mount up and ride out for you myself."

"Thanks, but you know I need you here."

And so did his little girlfriend. I couldn't let her get in the way. There were much bigger issues at hand—like the two hundred vampires I currently had traveling all over the city to find Gage.

There were only a few stragglers hanging behind, talking over their plans for how they'd spread out once they reached the surface. I wandered around, listening, taking it all in. It felt good, knowing I had smarts on my side. These were experienced vampires, the sort who'd seen war before and knew how to conduct things. A good leader was only as good as the people—or vampires—they trusted. I was learning more and more all the time.

I noticed one figure in particular, standing at the back of the room. He wore a hoodie, with the hood pulled over his head, and had his back to me—big, broad-shouldered. I approached.

"Excuse me," I said, raising one hand to touch his shoulder.

He turned.

Those eyes. Those damned eyes.

"What are you doing here? How did you get in?" I whispered.

Vance's piercing gaze drank me in. "I have my ways."

"Oh, I'm sure." I folded my arms, glaring at him.

"Don't I? I mean, I'm here, aren't I? So, I must know something."

"Right." I looked back and forth to be sure we weren't overheard. "I need you to leave. Now."

"Why?"

"Are you serious? They'll kill you just for being here. I don't know how you got in, and, frankly, I'm a little unsettled by this. We're not your clan. You don't belong."

"I know. But I thought I could help you."

Help me? I wouldn't let him do his sweet-talking routine. I had fallen for that too many times already. "You're delusional," I spat. "You need to leave."

"I know where Gage is."

My eyes locked onto his, and there might as well have not been another being in the assembly room—in the whole building, even. I could hardly breathe.

"You know? And you haven't told me yet?"

"You didn't exactly give me the chance yet," he uttered.

"I have to know if you're serious. I have to know you're not playing with me."

"I'm not playing. Look into my eyes. You know I'm telling the truth. I would never lie to you about something this important."

And the thing was, I knew he was right. He would never lead me on when it was something as important as what we were currently facing.

Cheating on me? That was one thing. But even he had a moral code—of sorts—when it came to things like finding my brother.

I didn't get the chance to ask where he was and what we had to do to save him.

Sledge beat me to anything I was about to say with the roar that came out of him when he saw us together.

I turned in the direction of the sound, my head snapping around, just in time to see a tall, dark blur flying at us.

No, at Vance.

Sledge's claws were extended, his fangs bared. He was ready to tear Vance into pieces.

Except, Vance wasn't simply any vampire, either. He was equally as strong as Sledge and twice as fast—Sledge had a lot of muscle and bulk, but it made him slow. After Vance hit the wall Sledge threw him into, he seemed to bounce off it and throw himself against Sledge. It was like that for a while as they flung each other back and forth, breaking tables and chairs, punching holes in walls, sending plaster through the air as they cracked the concrete of the floor.

"Stop this! Now! I mean it! We don't have time for this!"

I might as well have been talking to myself.

A group of two dozen vampires returned when they heard the noise—who could've missed it? They bared their fangs as soon as they saw it was Vance—a vampire from another clan— who fought with Sledge.

"No. This isn't happening." I pushed them back, into the tunnel. "I'll take care of this." I closed the doors, then closed the doors around the rest of the room to shut out anybody else who thought they'd join in the fight. I had enough problems.

I jumped up on the table again—the only table they hadn't yet broken.

"Stop this!" I bellowed, and my voice carried over the room. I could be good and loud when I needed to. I had to be, in a family full of boys. Being able to make myself heard meant I didn't get completely ignored while growing up.

They stopped, both of their heads turning toward me.

I wondered if they knew how ridiculous they looked, tangled up together on the floor, scratched and bleeding and panting like animals. "I want you to get off each other and move to opposite sides of the room. Now, before I call the others in here and let them deal with you. I think you'll like it better this way."

They shoved each other a few more times, but only half-heartedly. They both wanted to get the last word in, so to speak.

I rolled my eyes as they separated.

I swung around to Sledge. "Okay. I don't know why you think you can keep doing things like this."

"Me?" He pointed to himself, still breathing heavy. "Are you kidding?"

"No, I'm not. And if you knew me at all, you would know I'm not." I walked to him and put my hands on his shoulders. "Like I said, we had two dates. That was it. We're not a couple, Sledge. I'm sorry if I did or said something to give you the idea we were anything more."

He blinked once, twice, like he couldn't believe it. "You mean it."

"I do. And I think you need to think twice before you start anything like this again."

He shook me off, and I felt his fury as sure as if he'd hit me.

"Forget it. I thought you were worth protecting."

"I don't need your protection."

"That's what you think." He glared at Vance again.

"You leave me no choice but to ask you to go. I need you to leave, Sledge. Now."

He looked at me one more time, searching my face.

I wasn't about to budge—when he saw that, he stormed out of the room, throwing the doors open as he did. I saw others jumping out of his way as he stalked down the hall. He would've plowed right through them if they hadn't moved.

I turned to Vance with a heavy sigh.

He looked amused and maybe a little impressed with the way I'd handled myself.

As a matter of fact, I was impressed, too.

"All right. Take me to my brother."

❧ 15 ❧

JONAH

I was in a room that reminded me more of a tomb than anything else.

No windows, for one, so no light. My eyes worked just fine in the darkness, but it would've been nice to have some idea of where I was and what time of day it might be. The sensation of being totally separate from the rest of existence was unnerving. It could have been enough to drive me a little crazy.

I ran my hands over the solid rock walls, searching high and low for a way to escape. There had to be a seam, a crack, something I could use to jumpstart my escape.

All I found was a door which there was no prying open, no matter how I tried. Otherwise, the walls and floor were completely smooth. Even the seams where the walls met the floor were solid. The room had been carefully carved out of rock, the way the Sanctuary had. I could've still been at Sanctuary for all I knew. I didn't know where Steward had brought me.

"Come on," I growled, trying to pry the rock apart. I was a vampire, damn it. I should've been able to tear it to pieces with no trouble at all. Instead, all I did was tear my hands to pieces.

The pain was nothing in comparison to the way I felt about being trapped.

I needed to find Anissa. I needed to get us out of wherever we were. I couldn't wait for Steward to get here, since he might never get here at all. What would happen if one of the other Custodians found out he'd let us feed from him? What if they'd killed him for it? He would never come back. And I would be trapped forever. I couldn't let that happen.

I tried again to pry the door open, searching for the opening between the door and the doorframe. No luck. It was obviously under some sort of enchantment. I couldn't explain it any other way.

"What am I supposed to do?" I yelled, backing away from the door. The sound of my voice bounced off the walls, back and forth, until the room was filled with echoes. I waited for the sound to dissipate then sighed in frustration.

The door flew open with no warning, and a bright light flooded the room. I threw an arm over my eyes out of instinct since I was so acclimated to the darkness.

Once I lowered it, I watched in awe as a beautiful brunette walked into the room. The light around her reminded me of a halo. She was tall, willowy, and wore a white gown with gold embroidery throughout. Long, thick, wavy hair. Her eyes were the greenest emeralds, and her lips were full and ruby red. She was really something striking, which told me I had to be wary of her. Nothing so beautiful could be trusted. I didn't ask who she was or what she was doing here. She might be able to take something I said and turn it against me.

"My, my, my. All this noise you're making in here." She shook her head, clicking her tongue against her teeth. "You really shouldn't be such a noisy guest."

When she saw I wasn't about to let her pull me into her word games, she shrugged. "You're probably wondering how I know you're here. Isn't that right?"

Again, I didn't say a word. I only watched as she watched me.

She was trying hard to size me up. She wanted to know what she'd be able to get out of me.

I didn't want to play. I wanted to get out of here, and the door was still open. I couldn't let her know I was only waiting for the right moment to force my way past her and out into the... whatever was beyond the room.

"So. A Custodian and a vampire," she murmured, her eyes taking a long, casual tour of me.

I withstood it because I knew there was no other choice. I waited while she got an eyeful.

"What's a Custodian doing with a vampire, anyway?"

"What's a Custodian doing with a witch?" I fired back.

Her eyes widened, but only a fraction and only for a split second. "Well done. You're smarter than I gave you credit for. You want to know what Steward was doing with me?" She looked both ways comically then leaned a little closer. "I'm his dirty little secret."

"His what?"

"Well, I *was* his dirty little secret, anyway. I'm a former dirty little secret." She laughed a little, but there was no humor in that laugh. "So he's not with me, per se. Not anymore."

"Custodians aren't allowed to associate with witches," I said, like she needed to be reminded. I was only stalling, trying to get her off her guard.

She was so close to the door, but I could overpower her even with torn up hands.

"They're not allowed to associate with vampires, either, but here you are. I guess Steward isn't much for following the rules, is he?" She shrugged.

In another world, I wouldn't have minded her sense of humor. However, she was a witch, and we weren't exactly friends, either. I didn't trust witches. And, for some reason, I especially didn't trust her.

I needed to find Anissa. Right away. I had wasted so much time already. She could be terrified, hurting, in pain perhaps. I couldn't let that keep happening. She needed me.

"It's been nice visiting," I said, "but it's time for me to go now." I barreled across the room, past where she stood beside the door.

In the back of my mind I wondered why she didn't try to stop me... until an unseen force caught me and threw me backward across the room. I hit the opposite wall with a bone-crunching crash then slid to the floor.

"Not so fast, vampire." She sounded victorious as she watched me get to my feet.

I bared my fangs. "What do you think you're doing?"

"I'm keeping you where I want you," she replied coolly. "And if you think there's anything you can do about it, I'd ask you not to forget that magic trumps the so-called strength of the vampire, so don't waste your time."

"Don't mess with me," I warned. "You're starting something you don't want to finish. Trust me on this."

Her laugh was like the sound of bells chiming. How could anything so enchanting be so poisonous?

"Don't threaten me. Your threats mean nothing."

A portal opened beside me, and, before I could fight it, it pulled me through.

16

ANISSA

"I can't believe this. I mean, could that have gone any worse?" I paced back and forth while a very unconscious Steward laid on the ground at my feet.

"You've already said that—many times." Allonic raised a brow.

"I'm aware of that, thank you very much. I don't need you to tell me how many times I've said something."

"It's not helping things, so why do you keep saying it?"

"Because it's better than screaming or wringing your neck," I muttered.

"You could try."

Already Allonic and I were fighting like brother and sister. I wondered if he saw the irony there. It could've been he didn't know what siblings sounded like when they argued, since he didn't know what it was like to have one. He didn't have Sara or me in his life.

"Here." Allonic tore a strip of cloth from his robe and handed it to me. "There's a brook nearby."

"I hear it." And I knew what he meant, too. I wet the cloth in the brook then returned to wipe Steward's face with it.

Steward didn't flinch. No reaction at all.

"Boy," I muttered. "You really did a job on him."

"I thought I was doing it to help you," Allonic reminded me.

"Why did you?" I asked. "I mean, he's a Custodian, like you. Why would you attack him like that?"

"I did it for you, of course."

"But aren't you risking an awful lot? We don't really know each other."

"But we share a mother," he said, and his voice was softer than I'd ever heard it. "I feel like I owe it to her. I know she would want me to help you."

His words touched me deeply. "Thank you for that. I know I haven't genuinely thanked you yet. But thank you."

"You're welcome."

An uncomfortable silence stretched, filling in the empty space between us. In that silence was a million questions. A million and a half. I wondered if he would ever tell me what I needed to know. It couldn't have been easy for him, knowing I was there, maybe even on our mother's mind when she was with him. Nothing could've been easy on him—especially being half-vampire, since the Custodians didn't associate with vampires.

"I know you want to know more about her," he uttered.

"You need to stay out of my head."

"I wasn't in your head. Not like before, anyway. It was more like... well, I just know you want to know. I'd want to know, too. Besides, you're slightly single-minded. You don't let things go until you get what you want."

"Is that something our mother told you?"

"No. It's something I figured out about you pretty quickly."

"I see." I needed to stop asking him questions about her, especially questions which involved me.

"Why don't you feed from me? It'll give you all the answers you need."

The thought was a tempting one—extremely tempting. I wanted to know more than anything. Then, I remembered what it felt like to feed from Steward. What an unnerving memory. I would have to go through that again.

"Can't you tell me?"

"The short answer is no. It would take too long. You'll be able to see and understand more by experiencing my memories—and not merely my memories, but the shared memories of all the Custodians."

"I see."

It made sense. I wanted to know more about what happened after the Great Fire, especially. And why she'd decided never to come back to me—which hurt a lot more than I wanted to admit to myself. Why wasn't I enough for her to come back to? Sure, she had her reasons. She must have. But wasn't I reason enough to at least send word to let me know she was alive?

"All right," I decided. "I'll do it."

He offered me his wrist, and I took it in my hand. I was much smaller than him, and his hand dwarfed mine. I looked up at him, and he nodded once. I was about to feed for the second time that day—or maybe the third, since I didn't know exactly when I'd fed from Steward in relation to the present moment.

I bared my fangs and sank them into his wrist. The first rush flooded me, almost like a wave crashing through me and filling me with a blast of euphoria. It took concentration—all I had—to keep from losing control and drinking deep to make the feeling last as long as possible.

The memories came quickly, flashing past my eyes as I drank. There she was again. My mother. Our mother. She was burned almost beyond recognition and clearly in terrible pain. Every movement was almost enough to send her into convulsions, but she crawled anyway. And kept crawling. The sun burned her worse than the fire had, and she searched for cover in vain.

A Custodian came to her rescue—his robes were a giveaway. He carried her into the Sanctuary, where he laid her down and allowed her to feed. Her burns were deep, so deep. She fed, and, as she did, the Custodian shared memories with her.

Years passed. She looked healthier, her skin as healed as it could be after she'd suffered the way she had. And her skin changed, too. She no longer had the same pale skin all vampires shared. It darkened the longer she fed. She was never as dark as the rest of the shades, but she was still markedly different than I remembered her.

I saw her take the Custodian who'd helped her as a mate. She loved him. I could feel it. And he loved her. She was his secret, and he had protected her for so long. She would be dead if it weren't for him. So they were in love and they had a baby. Allonic. She loved him, too. She was good to him, even if he had to stay hidden the way she did. After all, a surprise baby wouldn't have worked. He would've given them away. He'd grown up there in the Sanctuary, barely allowed to interact with the others.

Mom loved to sketch. That was one thing I remembered about her, the art she used to create. She created sketch after sketch of little girls. Me and Sara. I wished I could wrap my arms around her and hug her, and tell her I was thinking about her, too. That I missed her.

I pulled away from Allonic, unable to see any more. Tears streamed down my face. She'd thought about me and Sara. She had wanted us. She had spent years and years in a cave, trying to heal. It was all too much to take.

"Your father and my mother," I whispered.

"Our mother," he corrected.

"Yes. I'm sorry. I didn't mean to ignore you. It's a habit, thinking of her as only mine. And Sara's."

He nodded then looked back down at Steward. "Did he tell you we're related?"

"He did. Your father was his cousin."

"That's right."

"Who was your father, though? Did you know him well?"

He shrugged. "As well as I could, considering I wasn't supposed to exist."

"I'm sorry for that. I sort of know how that feels, at least a little. None of the vampires in my clan accepted me, since I wasn't full-blood." And at least he had my mother to love him. I didn't have anybody but Sara. I couldn't say that out loud.

"My grandfather is leader, and that leadership would've gone over to my father."

"Where is he?"

"He's gone."

"I see," I whispered. "Does that mean you'll be the leader one day?"

"Funny you should ask," he sneered. "No. My grandfather would never hand over leadership to a half-vampire. He hates me. There are even a few in the Sanctuary actively against my leading."

"Oh." I didn't know what else to say. We had more in common than I'd originally thought.

We sat in silence for a little while before another pretty obvious question sprang to mind. "Do you feed? I mean, the way I feed?"

He shook his head. "I have fangs," he explained, and he bared them for me.

It was disquieting, seeing a shade with fangs.

"But I have no bloodlust. I can survive without it."

I nodded.

"Being a half-blood... It's not easy. You never feel like you fully fit in on one side or the other."

"I know, I know. Like I said, I've felt that pain. I always wondered why the rest of my clan shunned me. I wondered why I was a little different from the rest of them. Now I know it was because of my fae blood. And my father, well, he expects me to relinquish all vampire ties and join him. Like I could ever forget half of myself." Something occurred to me. "Our mother. When she drank your father's blood... Steward said it changed her. I saw the way her skin tone changed. Did anything else change?"

"You mean, was she still a vampire?"

"Right."

He waited a long time before answering, and I held my breath in anticipation.

"No," he finally replied in a quiet voice. "She would never stop being vampire, you understand, but after feeding from my father for so many years, his blood changed what she needed. The way I'm still half-vampire but have no need for blood. It was the same for her."

I felt a sadness I couldn't describe. I didn't know why I should be sad. My mother had survived. She hadn't only survived, but had found love again. And she'd had a baby to love, too. But she'd lost part of herself in the process—and she'd lost her daughters.

Why didn't she ever reach out? I knew it was something Allonic's memories could never show me. She must've had a reason, deep down in her heart.

For some reason, I thought of Gregor, my father and leader of the fae. My heart ached for him, too. I needed a parent. I had so many feelings to process, and, yes, I knew I was old enough to deal with them on my own. I shouldn't have needed their guidance, but a little advice and understanding would have been nice. I'd never felt so alone.

I missed Gregor. It was so strange. How could I miss somebody I barely knew? But I did. I wished I hadn't shut him out. I was sure he'd be too angry with me to ever accept my apology. Too angry and too disappointed.

I opened my mouth to tell Allonic how I felt—but when Steward sat up and lunged for Allonic, anything I would've said was lost to the melee that ensued.

17

ANISSA

"Stop this!" I fell backward from where I'd been crouching beside Steward, pushed aside when he went for Allonic's throat. Just as I had threatened to do not long before then.

I watched as they scuffled, rolling back and forth across the ground, grunting and growling and hurling what I was sure was curses in another language at each other. Steward did most of the cursing, really. I could only imagine how furious he was.

"Stop, I said!" I took my life in my hands by throwing myself between them. "Please! We don't have time for this. Settle it later." I got up, brushed myself off, and was deeply relieved when the other two followed along.

"Where is Jonah?" I asked Steward. "Please. We have to get to him."

He nodded while rubbing the back of his head. "You're right. I'll take you to him, but we need to port."

"Okay. Let's do it." Poor Jonah. He'd been waiting for so long for me. He had to be frantic by now.

"I need to use a spiritwalker in order to take you there."

"Ha! Not a chance." I folded my arms.

"Excuse me?"

"Have you already forgotten what happened the last time you tried to use a spiritwalker on me?" I asked. "That's what got us into this situation—you with a lump on the back of your head."

"I can't just take you there. I don't want to run the risk—"

I rolled my eyes. "I know. You can't run the risk of my running away or doing something I shouldn't. While I don't blame you for not trusting me, I need you to believe I don't do things like that when the stakes are this high. I wouldn't do anything to jeopardize Jonah right now—or your security. I swear."

"I'll bring her with me," Allonic offered. "I'll take care of her as we cross over. You don't have to be concerned."

Steward shot him a deadly look. "We have a lot to settle."

"I know we do, but like she said, this isn't the time."

Steward let out something between a snarl and a sigh. "As you wish, then." He opened a portal, there in front of us.

It shimmered and shone, and I wondered what it must be like to have such power. To be able to open a portal anytime, anywhere, leading anyplace.

"Come." My heart took off at a gallop as Allonic pulled me under his cloak, pressing me close. I wrapped my arms around his waist and went with him, stepped as he stepped.

Just like that, the sounds of the forest were no more. No owls, no crickets, no bats. No breeze in the trees. Nothing. And no light, either. Allonic pulled his cloak away, and I found myself in a room as dark as it had been under the cloak.

The room was also empty. No Jonah.

"Where is he?" I looked from one of them to the other. "I thought he was here. You brought us here and said it was where Jonah was."

"Enough," Steward said. "Enough. I need to think." He was angry. Deeply, deeply angry.

I could feel it around him, like he wore an aura of anger. He walked to the open door carved into one wall then turned around. His face was set in tight, rigid lines.

I glanced around again, taking in the walls, their smoothness.

Almost supernaturally smooth. Who created it? How long ago was it created? And why did he choose this place, of all possible places, to store Jonah while he searched for me? I could imagine Jonah in there, all alone, wanting to find me but being trapped.

"What do you think happened?" Allonic asked.

"I don't know. How should I know? I left him here because I knew he would be safe here. No one ever comes here. It's all but forgotten."

A high-pitched laugh, one which reminded me of the chiming of bells, rang throughout the room. But instead of making me smile, it sent a cold chill down my spine.

I turned to find where it had come from and saw Steward already knew. He stood at attention, every muscle in his body tight.

"What are you doing here?" Steward muttered.

He wasn't talking to me. He was talking to the tall, willowy brunette who stepped out of the shadows.

She was beautiful. Stunning, actually. Her eyes glowed like green fire. They reminded me of Steward's in a way. Her ruby-red lips curved into a smile as she walked to him.

"Hello to you, too." She ran a fingertip along his jawline.

He growled dangerously before he recoiled like her touch burned.

"Where is Jonah? What have you done with him?"

She didn't answer his question, probably because she was too busy looking at me.

I felt her eyes burning into me, sizing me up. She had hurt Jonah. I was sure of it.

I glared at her, willing her to make a move if she thought she was strong enough. I might not win the fight, but she would remember me.

"Who's this?" she asked, pointing at me. "My replacement?"

Replacement? Suddenly, the finger down his jaw made sense. And I lost control. I don't know why. It might have been because she wasn't telling what she knew. It might've been because I was desperate at that point to find Jonah and make sure he was safe, with me, where he belonged. Maybe because I didn't like the way she looked at me and most definitely didn't like the way she pointed. No matter why, I threw myself at her for all I was worth.

Then, I was flying across the room and slamming into the wall behind me. I never reached her before she cast some sort of spell. She was a witch, without a doubt.

I didn't care. Instead of cowering against the wall the way she obviously wanted me to, I lunged at her again. This time I intended to rip her throat out if I had to. I must have taken her by surprise because I managed to get my hands around her neck. The force of our collision knocked her against the opposite wall.

Steward's hands clamped down on my shoulders and pulled me away. I roared in protest—I had to destroy her.

"Remember how you felt when I couldn't tell you the thing only I knew," he reminded me.

He referred to when he was unconscious and unable to tell me where Jonah was, and he was right. I relaxed, but only a little.

He turned his attention to the witch. "Where is Jonah, Marianelle?"

She only shrugged, which enraged me more. I lunged for her again, but Steward's grip held me back.

"Tell me," Steward continued. "Where is he?"

"Not here," she replied.

Oh, I wanted to kill her.

Evidently, Steward was starting to lose his patience—one of his hands left my shoulder and reached for her like he was about to inflict harm.

She flinched away from his grasp. "All right," she gasped. "His presence was desired."

"That's all?" I asked after she fell silent. "His presence was desired? That's not an answer, you disgusting bitch! And you know it! You know what he's asking and you deliberately play word games like this when you know we don't have the time!"

"Anissa," Steward warned. "Don't lose yourself like this."

"But she knows! I know she knows!"

"So do I," he replied in a deadly tone.

I looked up at him, and he stared at her.

I needed him to get through to her, and it wasn't working so far.

"Who desired his presence, Marianelle? And don't play with my words. Tell me. Who was it?"

All the while, Allonic stood off to the side with a detached expression on his face. He hadn't said a word until then. It almost surprised me when he cleared his throat.

"Fane," Allonic said.

❧ 18 ❧

I never knew anger had a scent before, but the smell hung heavy in the air as I stared at Vance.

The overhead lighting still worked—they hadn't broken that, though they probably would have if I hadn't stopped them—and it cast part of Vance's face in shadow. I wished I knew what he was thinking. Didn't I already wish that before?

"I mean it," I said. "I need to find my brother, and I need you tell me how."

"It's not that easy."

"I don't see why not. I mean, before I saw you standing there, I would've thought it was impossible to get in here if you weren't a Bourke. But here you are. You have your ways, right?"

He smirked. "This goes beyond a little sneaking around."

"All right. So what happened, really? Do you know or not? Telling me where he is and actually taking me to him are two different things."

We circled each other like wary predators, eyeing each other up as we did. The fight with Sledge hadn't hurt him one bit—I remembered the abrasions and bruises on Sledge's face.

Vance looked like he could go another few rounds if it came down to it.

I raised one eyebrow as I frowned at him. "Unless you're too much of a punk to follow through on your promises."

"I didn't promise you anything. I didn't have the chance. We were interrupted, remember?"

"How could I forget? I'm the one who has to pay for the damage."

A rueful grin spread across his handsome face. "Sorry about that."

"Let's not change the subject." But it was so easy to when I was with him. It was exhilarating, matching wits with somebody at least mostly as intelligent as me. It had been too long. What I missed most about him was his mind. I had always loved talking with him, playing word games, bantering. Sometimes, it was hotter than anything else we ever got up to.

"Oh, right. You wanted to know about Gage."

We stopped circling and stood still.

"Yes. I want to know who kidnapped him."

"That's easy." He folded his arms. "Nobody."

"What?" My jaw nearly hit the floor.

"He hasn't been kidnapped. He's hiding."

I had to sit down. I found the nearest chair they hadn't broken and sank into it. "Hiding?" I asked breathlessly. "From what? From whom? And where?"

"First thing's first." He pulled up another chair, turning it around backward and straddling it in front of me. His tall, strong, sure body moved as gracefully as a cat's.

It wasn't easy to pry my eyes from him and focus my thoughts.

He raised a brow, then said, "I know this because it was my father Gage went to."

"Lucian?"

That was almost more shocking than finding out he was hiding. Why would he go to the head of the league for sanctuary? What had he done? Or what was he afraid of having done to him?

Vance leaned closer, and it took a feat of will to push away any lingering feelings I had for him. I tried, hard, to tell myself there was nothing between us, but that wasn't strictly the truth. I still cared for him. More than cared. I wanted him. Being near him was enough to send my body into overdrive, even when my brain was consumed with other things.

Now, I couldn't control the way he made my pulse speed up. I couldn't keep my skin from tingling. I only wished I could. I hated he was able to break me down like this.

"Yeah. He went to my father and said he needed help. That's all I know."

"And this was when?"

"Not long ago. Between the league meeting and now."

"After the bloodbath," I murmured, remembering the horror I had seen. As a vampire, I was used to the sight of blood. Still, what I'd seen in that room had turned my stomach. I wouldn't forget it anytime soon. "He must have been running from whatever happened."

He shrugged. "I don't know about any of that."

"He's safe, then?" That was something, anyway.

"Yes. For now. At league headquarters."

And I had just been there. We had probably crossed paths. "Poor Gage. He must be terrified, taking a risk like that. Going to your father. I mean, nobody does that. It isn't done, Vance."

"You don't need to tell me that." He snickered.

"Well, I have to see him." I stood, resolute.

"That's not going to happen." He stood, too, and reminded me how much taller he was than me. I refused to back down in front of him. I wouldn't let him intimidate me.

"Oh, no?"

"Listen. This is great and everything, the way you want to save your brother, but it's not a good idea. If I lead you to him, my father will know it was me who did it."

"Oh, and you wouldn't want to get your father upset, would you?"

He frowned, deep lines creasing his forehead. His icy eyes

hardened. "You know I don't want to, and I don't appreciate the way you're trying to make it sound like a joke, either."

"All right, all right." I held up my hands. "I didn't know he had you under his thumb like this." I stepped backward, shaking my head.

He only chuckled. "You think you're so smart, don't you? Like you can talk me into anything by using that reverse psychology stuff."

I shrugged. "It's not like it hasn't worked before. I remember more than once being able to talk to you into things you didn't want to do at first."

"Yeah, well maybe I wanted to do them all along but wanted to know how much you wanted me to do them."

"That... makes no sense."

He laughed. "You know what I'm trying to say."

"Has anything between us ever been completely honest? I mean, no games, no word play, no testing? Just... us?" Where had that come from? I guessed I needed to know if I was willing to blurt it out like that.

"Sure. Don't you remember?" He took one step closer to me, then another.

Damn him.

He knew how to tear me between wanting more and wanting him to stop.

My heart raced and my blood hummed, and I very much wanted to know what he had in mind, thought my brain told me it was the stupidest idea anyone could ever have and I needed to run screaming from the room before things went too far.

"I'm afraid I don't," I whispered, hoping he wouldn't choose to remind me.

"Well, we'll have to do something about that." He backed me into the wall.

I slid past him, walking to the center of the room. I heard his dry chuckle behind me.

"I don't think we need to. We don't have a lot of time, after all, and I need to see my brother whether you plan on helping me get to him or not." I grinned, turning to face him. "Come on. You know me. You know I'll leave as soon as I'm free of you and course straight to the cathedral."

"You would, too, wouldn't you?" He shook his head, grinning. "Absolutely."

"I'm afraid I'm going to need something in return, then."

"Oh, come on. You mean you won't do me a favor for old time's sake? You don't think you owe me that much, at least?" I shook my head. "I'm disappointed in you."

"Old time's sake doesn't mean much to me—no offense. What I care about is the here and now, as in the fact we are both right here, right now." He smiled, approaching again.

And again, I backed away—only this time, when he pinned me against the wall, I didn't try to get past him. The dangerous side of me, the side he'd always managed to unleash, wanted to see where this would go.

He smiled victoriously, like he had me right where he wanted me—trapped, nowhere to go, no way to resist him.

And his smile snapped something inside me. In a flash, my fangs were bared. I pushed him away from me.

"You want to know what you get in return? You get to live. How's that sound? I could just as easily call my clan in to take care of you for me."

He was too fast for me, taking my wrists in his much larger hands, holding them above my head. "I want a kiss."

"Get out of here," I spat, turning my face away, even as my heart raced and I struggled to breathe.

"Come on," he whispered. "You used to enjoy my kisses."

I wriggled, trying to free myself. "Yeah, well, I didn't have many good qualities to choose from, did I?" The hoodie he wore barely concealed his strong, hard body, but when I inadvertently pressed myself against him as I fought to be free, my knees went a little weak.

"One little kiss. What could it hurt?"

"Plenty, and you know it. Let go of me, damn you!" I threw my body against his, hoping to knock him off-balance. No such luck. All it did was get me more flustered, which was the last thing I needed.

"Am I really so repulsive?" I closed my eyes and shivered, cursing my heart for betraying me. His deep, throaty chuckle told me he knew what I was going through even as I struggled with him.

I had to do something, anything to make it stop. "Okay, fine. One kiss."

He straightened, looking down at me with surprise all over his face. "Really?"

"Really." I turned my face to the side. "A kiss on the cheek."

He laughed. "I guess I have to take what I'm given. I didn't specify the kind of kiss, after all—although you're the one who's losing out in the end."

I lowered my eyelids, keeping my emotions a secret, knowing I was probably failing, and hating how easy it was for him to manipulate me.

I was surprised to feel a soft kiss a moment later. It was sweet, gentle.

It made me smile.

The doors opened and in walked Sledge.

Of course.

He had impeccable timing. I pulled my wrists from Vance's hands, as the surprise of Sledge walking in had been enough to loosen his grip.

"Get your hands off her!" Sledge roared.

"His hands are off me!" I raised Vance's hands up. "See? He's not touching me anymore. Stop this. It's ridiculous."

"You think I'm gonna be okay with watching him paw you like that? I know you don't think we're anything, Philippa, but I have more respect for you than that."

Right. That was why he made a fool of me in front of everyone by pointing out my smudged lip gloss.

"Knock it off. I mean it. I'm sick of this, so you might as well drop it." I looked at Vance, who was clearly ready to fight again. "Come on. We're going, now that you've been paid up."

"Going where?" Sledge asked, fists clenched at his sides.

In any other situation, it would have been flattering to see two guys fighting over me. I'd seen it before, actually. More than once. And I'd always liked it. Just not so much right at the moment.

"Tell Scott I've gone to get Gage," I ordered. "And no, I don't need you to come with me." He was worse than an overzealous guard dog.

❧ 19 ❧

JONAH

The ground was cold and hard beneath me. I couldn't shake the fog in my head right away—getting thrown through a portal wasn't easy, and the witch hadn't been gentle with me, either.

I took a deep breath, then another. The air was cold, too, and damp. I was tired of dampness—we didn't feel it the way humans did, but it still wasn't pleasant.

I could hardly see my hand in front of my face. A mist covered the ground, cloaking everything. Otherwise, it was dark.

Pitch black.

Even my vampire eyes could hardly make out the shapes around me. Large, looming shapes. I couldn't quite tell what they were.

I took a chance and stood up, glancing around. I kept my ears tuned in to any sound, but all I heard was the beating of my heart and the sound of my breath. Maybe the mist deadened any other sound on the ground.

One step, then another, I came closer to one of those hulking shapes. They didn't move, any of them. I realized what they were. The backs of mausoleums.

I was in a graveyard.

Shapeless forms became angels, gazing down at me with their stone eyes. Condemning me.

I made out the tops of headstones, the iron doors of one family crypt after another.

At least I knew I was in a graveyard. But I didn't know where or why I'd been brought here. Or how I'd get back, for that matter. What was the purpose of any of it? And to think, I'd been so sure hiding in the Sanctuary would mean Anissa and I would be safe for a little while.

I heard a sound, like a footstep over stone. I fell into a fighting stance, one foot behind the other, claws extended. I had no idea what to expect, or who. Had the witch sent me here to kill me?

Another footstep, then another. They were coming from behind a crumbling tomb roughly twenty feet from where I stood, a sprawling thing that must have been built for a very wealthy family. It might have been whole and impressive centuries earlier but had fallen into disrepair, much like everything around me. Anything could be lurking there in the mist. I readied myself for whatever was coming.

When I saw exactly what was approaching, I let out a shuddery breath. It felt like I'd been kicked in the stomach by a horse. All the air left my lungs. I felt sick.

When I was finally able to speak, I said only one word to the man who'd stepped out from behind the tomb.

"You."

The word echoed off the walls of the other tombs and monuments, almost an accusation.

You, you, you.

He nodded in the darkness. "Son."

I couldn't believe my eyes.

He didn't appear much older than he had when I last saw him —of course, he wouldn't. We didn't age quickly, after all, and I only looked a year or two older in human terms than I had on the day my parents disappeared. All those years ago. Wondering where he was. No answers, no clues, nothing. Hoping for the best but only able to believe the worst. After all, wouldn't a parent let their child know he was still alive? I'd let go of hope a long time before then, needing to take over and lead the clan. I couldn't lose myself in worry and doubt, could I?

"What happened?" I managed to sputter, reeling a little, swaying on my feet. His appearance gave the impression he'd been through a war. His eyes were tired, lined. That was what had changed most about him, I decided. He'd always been so youthful, both in his smooth, young face and his shining eyes. Those eyes didn't shine or twinkle as he stared at me.

"It's a long story," he murmured.

Like that was enough of an explanation. It wasn't enough, not at all. Nothing would ever be enough to fill all the emptiness he'd left.

"And Mom?" I couldn't help hoping again. If he was here, she might be, too.

But he shook his head, eyes lowering a little.

Fresh pain pierced me, as real and raw as it was the day they disappeared. It was like losing her all over again, the confirmation she was really gone. She would never come back. Knowing I would never see her face again, never see her smile, was like a knife in me. A white-hot knife, silver, burning me from the inside out.

I took a deep breath, closing my eyes for a second to steady myself. There was too much to ask, too much to learn, to let myself fall into despair.

"Would you like to tell me where you've been all this time? Do you think I deserve to know?" I looked him over.

He wore a long, gray coat—or maybe it wasn't gray, but it appeared that way in the near-perfect darkness. Underneath was a button-down shirt that had seen better days and a pair of those cargo pants with all the pockets that humans loved so much. Leather boots on his feet, battered, dirty.

He emanated a power I didn't remember him having. It was almost tangible. What had he been through? Where had he gone?

"Not that you don't deserve or didn't deserve." His voice was still the same, wasn't it? That same evenly measured tone. The same warmth. Yet, I heard fatigue in it, too. A soul-weary exhaustion. "It's only that I was trying to protect you."

"Protect me? From what? From whom?"

"Things you didn't need to know about. Things I would still rather you not know about, only my hand has been pressed. I've had no choice but to reach out to you, though I can't afford to be found." He shook his head. "I couldn't afford to let you know anything about me. It would put you in jeopardy."

"About you? What could you possibly have done I wouldn't be able to know about?"

He had always been the strongest, most honorable of all the Bourke clan. I had looked up to him, idolized him. He was my ideal from the time I was old enough to have one. In the years since he'd disappeared, I'd done everything I could to pattern myself after him. And all he could tell me was there were secrets I wasn't supposed to know about?

"It's not what I've done, so much as what they say I've done."

"Who's they?"

He shook his head, appearing more tired than ever. "It's enough to say I had to go rogue," he murmured. "There was no other choice. It was for your safety, your protection—just like it's for your protection now that I hesitate in telling you what needs to be said. It's dangerous, but it would be far more dangerous if I let things go as they are."

"Gone rogue?" I couldn't imagine it. He must have traveled deep underground to keep himself away from those who would recognize him. He was one of the most revered clan leaders of his day. I wondered what it had been like for him for all those years, hiding, going from place to place in hopes no one could identify him. Keeping away from us.

He nodded. "I'm no longer Dommik Bourke," he said, and there was such grief in his voice I could hardly stand it.

"You're not?" I felt like an idiot, standing there asking questions.

"I haven't been Dommik Bourke in a very long time. Not since I left you and your brothers and sister. Since then, I've gone by another name. One you may have heard over the years." He took a deep breath, like he was pausing for effect. Or giving me a chance to steel myself for what was to come. "I'm known as Fane."

No wonder he had given me a chance to prepare. I was stunned, speechless, almost horrified.

Fane.

A name everyone in our world knew. Like one of the super-heroes humans cared so much about.

He was a legend, one that moved only under the cover of darkness. A name to be feared, to be respected. One usually spoken only in whispers.

"You're Fane? How is it possible? I mean... I mean, Fane is... He's like a myth. He's a legend. He has power unlike the rest of us. And that's... you?"

He nodded. "It's all true."

"They also say he's... you're solitary."

"Also true."

"And that he set fire to the Carver clan and fled."

"That's not true," he smoothly fired back.

Hope bloomed inside me. "Who, then?"

"Someone who set the fire then pointed an accusatory finger in our clan's direction." His voice was tinged with the pain of betrayal, though so many years had passed.

I couldn't make sense of it. "They still think we did it. So, why did you have to flee? I mean, we've survived the accusations. No, we're not allied with the Carvers, but..."

"But if I had stayed, you wouldn't be in the position you're in. Trust me." He sighed, leaning against the crumbling marble. "If your mother and I had stayed, the entire clan would have been in trouble—but especially you kids. I couldn't let you suffer that sort of danger. Your mother and I had to leave. There was no other choice."

He stared off into the distance, almost as if he could look into the past. "Elena didn't want to go away, but she knew, no matter the pain it caused her, there would be more pain if you suffered because we'd stayed. She wanted to leave word, too. I did as well. But there was no way. Any clue we gave you as to our whereabouts could've led to us. And it could have put you in danger."

"What about years later, once everything calmed down? I could see wanting to stay away while the fire was still a fresh memory, but now? You couldn't have sent word, reached out somehow, to let us know you were alive?"

I was desperately glad he wasn't dead—nothing would change that—but I couldn't get the pain and the relief to coexist peacefully. The pain kept coming back, along with memories of aching for my parents every day, my imagination going wild as I pictured what might have happened to them. Nothing in real life could've been worse than what I held in my imagination.

"If anybody knew I was alive there would have been trouble. Deadly trouble. It was better for everyone to think I was dead. If I was alive, you would all be perceived as threats."

"I don't understand."

"If it was known I had survived, others might think I could work through you. That I could lead the clan through you. There would be a question of whether you were doing my bidding, carrying on my legacy. I couldn't have that, don't you see? It was painful for me, and doubly painful for your mother, but that was how it had to be. I'll always believe that."

He sounded again like the honorable father I had remembered for so long. Someone who would make a supreme sacrifice for the sake of those he loved.

"If there's so much danger, why did you summon me now?"

He grimaced. "I was tempted when I first heard of the tension brewing between you and your brother."

How was it that, even after so many decades of existence and so many of them without my father, I could still feel guilty when he used that tone of voice? The disappointment was almost palpable.

He continued. "And then again, I heard you'd left your rightful position and gone rogue yourself." He shook his head. "That was very foolhardy."

"I know, but I made my decision with a clear head."

His jaw tightened. "That's neither here nor there at the moment," he muttered. "Finally, the last straw came when I heard about some detective work your brother has been doing."

"Gage?"

He nodded. "It seems he's delivered himself into a precarious situation, thanks to his sleuthing."

"What do you mean?"

He sighed, shaking his head. "Lucian."

20

JONAH

"Lucian? What does he have to do with any of this?" The more he spoke, the more confused I became. It was like listening to riddles, on and on.

"Plenty. And your brother has gone straight to him."

"But why? What could he have learned that would make him do that?"

"I'm not sure," he admitted. "I only know he's in trouble now."

Should I care? I told myself I should, but it wasn't easy to stir up any concern. Still, if my father—Fane, I corrected myself—thought it was worth reaching out to me after so many years, there must have been a real threat.

"How are you aware of so much?" I asked. "You've gone rogue. How do you know about the problems I had with Gage? How do you know about my leaving the clan?"

He smiled a little. "I may have gone rogue among the vampires, but I haven't cut off communication with all creatures. I managed to find a way to make myself indispensable to a high-ranking witch or two. Maybe a few other types of supernaturals."

I didn't want to know how he'd managed to do that. Certain things a son didn't want to know about his father.

"Thanks to witches," he continued, "I get access to perks like the Passages."

"Passages?"

He nodded. "A series of interconnecting paths which occasionally use portals to connect. Like underground, but not. Just a different dimension."

There was still so much to know, so much I wasn't aware of. Had I ever been a solid leader when I was in dark about so much? Had I been kidding myself all along? Portals connecting different dimensions. I guessed I was somewhere along one of those paths he'd talked about.

"So that was how I got here," I murmured.

He nodded. "Yes, I was sure this was somewhere you wouldn't be discovered with me."

"Who was the witch who sent me here? One of the ones you're so indispensable to?"

His face was blank, unreadable.

I wasn't about to press him for more information. I didn't want to know.

Thinking about the witch made me think about trying to get out of that sealed-up room, trying to get back to Anissa.

Anissa.

She was still out there somewhere. I had to find her.

"I need to get back to where I came from," I said, suddenly in a hurry to go.

But I didn't want to leave him, either. Not after so long apart, not when there were so many more unanswered questions between us. I could hardly stand it. Still, there was no choice.

He should understand, I thought, considering that years earlier, he didn't want to go, but had no choice. He had to do what he thought was right. "How can I find you later?"

He sneered. "What's the rush? Eager to return to the half-br—"

"Don't." I stared him down. "Don't call her that."

So what if he was the legendary Fane? I wouldn't let him talk about Anissa that way. I wouldn't let anybody do that.

He nodded slightly. "And what about your brother? What about Gage?"

"What about him?"

"Don't you want to know more?"

I shook my head. "He abandoned the clan and rebelled against my leadership. If you know what happened, then you must know about that."

He absorbed that without moving or even blinking. Whether or not he understood, I didn't know. He kept his thoughts on the matter to himself. A born leader, he knew when to stay silent.

"I'll take you back to the place Marianelle brought you from. You can't return without a witch who knows—"

"Understood." Irritated, I was tired of waiting. I was tired of talking about Gage. I needed to find Anissa. She was all that mattered.

A small smile played along the corners of Fane's mouth as he threw a portal quicker than I could see him do it. It was so close to me, I didn't have to move in order for it to pull me in. I didn't get the chance to say anything to him. Not even goodbye.

In the blink of an eye, I crash-landed in a dark room with stone floors. The same dark room as before.

So, he had sent me back, as promised. I should've known he would. I could still trust him after all this time.

"Jonah!"

I looked up to find Anissa staring at me, mouth open in shock. I got to my feet and took in the sight of not only her, but also Steward and the witch—Marianelle, Fane had called her.

I had to remind myself to think of him that way.

He wasn't my father.

He was Fane.

And then, standing nearby, there was Anissa's brother. All of them, together.

But Anissa was the one I focused on. And the first thing I noticed was how terrible she looked. Like she'd been buried alive.

I hurried to her side. "Are you okay?"

There was dirt all over her face and clothes. Her nails were filthy, packed with sod. There were leaves and small twigs in her hair—I picked a few of them out. Not only that, either. I saw abrasions, blood. She'd been fighting. Who? I berated myself for leaving her alone to take care of herself. I couldn't imagine what she'd been through.

"Are you?" Her hand trembled as she touched my face.

"I'm fine."

"Me, too."

What a relief. I could relax for the first time since she'd disappeared.

"Where were you?" she asked.

I felt Marianelle's eyes on me. She knew where I was, of course. She wouldn't tell, and I couldn't. I couldn't put anyone—especially Anissa—in danger that way.

Especially not Anissa.

I gave her what I hoped was a smile that would put her mind at ease. "Rest assured I'm all right. There's nothing to worry about."

As a second thought, I turned to where I'd first fallen into the room. The portal was gone. Fane hadn't followed me through. How would I find him again?

21

PHILIPPA

It took less than half an hour before Vance and I reached the cathedral at the League of Vampires. It felt like I had just been there, maybe because I had. And there was Gage, sneaking in after I had already left. He never had great timing, my brother.

The spires of the cathedral climbed toward the sky, and from the many windows lining the great building came a soft glow.

"Someone's in there," I murmured as Vance and I approached.

"Of course," he chuckled. "Somebody's always in there. There's at least one guard on duty at all times."

"How will we get in if they're watching I don't think we can simply walk up and knock. Or can we?"

He snickered. "No. I don't think that would be a good idea. Come on. I have a better way."

Instead of leading me to the front entrance, which we'd used for the meeting, Vance snuck around the side of the building to a series of windows along the back. It must have been a basement of some sort when the building was used for its original intention.

"We're breaking in?" I asked, shocked.

"Not exactly." He bent down and, with the tip of one finger, delivered a series of taps against the glass.

As if by magic, the window swung open.

"After you," he said, motioning to the opening.

"You want me to go in through there?" I wasn't exactly keen on sliding in through a dirty, dusty old window. I might have been head of the clan and had to give up partying, but I still liked looking nice. Or not like a hobo, at least.

"Yeah, I do. If you want to see your brother again."

When I looked down again with a frown, I heard him sigh.

"Here. Wear this. Girls are the worst sometimes." He took off his hoodie.

I couldn't take my eyes off his strong, broad body as he handed it over.

I wrapped it around my waist, covering my legs and butt to protect my clothes before sliding through the window and into the basement. I heard Vance following me.

There was a figure in the shadows, one I recognized.

"Gage." I rushed to him, nearly crashing into him as I threw my arms around his neck. "I would appreciate it if you never did anything like this again. All right?"

He hugged me back, but it was brief.

I felt the hesitation in him and knew there was plenty for him to tell me.

I turned to Vance, who waited by the window. "I think Gage and I should talk alone," I murmured.

He seemed annoyed, like he wanted me to thank him or at least give him the chance to hear what my brother had to say, but I didn't owe him anything. He climbed back out of the window.

"No, no, it can't be here. I don't trust this place." Gage glanced around.

I wondered if he was becoming a little paranoid. He had a haunted look about him. Well, could I blame him? He knew he was in danger. Exactly how much danger, only he knew.

"Where should we go?" I whispered.

"Away. To the forest. Anywhere." He helped me out through the window then followed me.

We went far into the woods, miles away from the cathedral until it was nothing more than a dot on the horizon. It didn't take long using our natural speed, though I was already weakened from coursing to the cathedral.

"All right," I said when he stopped. "I think we're safe out here, don't you?"

"I don't know where I'm safe," he admitted, fear in his voice. It felt like a hand clutched my heart and squeezed tight.

"What do you mean? What's happening?" I took him by the shoulders, staring up into his face. "I don't understand. You run off, and then you tell me you're afraid. Afraid of what? Why do you need to go to Lucian for protection?" I stepped away, suddenly understanding more than I did before. "What have you done that you need protecting?"

"I didn't do anything," he insisted. "Nothing, except find out more than I should have."

"About what? You know I don't like it when you're cryptic like this. We don't have much time."

He nodded. "I know."

"So, what is it? What do you know?"

He turned away, hands in his pockets. "You know about my group." He seemed to shudder a little when he said it.

"Yes," I whispered. "I saw it."

"So you know how vicious it was?"

"I do. I would run, too, if that happened to my group."

"I'm scared I'll be next."

"I don't blame you, but you can't stay here forever. What happens if you're discovered? What happens if Lucian doesn't want to involve himself any longer? I mean, if it's the Carvers doing this..."

He stiffened at the mention of the Carver name.

I watched him closely and took note of the way he wouldn't face me. "Why are you looking away?"

"I'm not."

"You are. Turn around and face me, then."

When he didn't, I knew.

"You're holding something back, aren't you?"

"No."

"Yes, you are. There's something you're not telling me."

"Maybe it's for the best that I don't."

I growled. "This is ridiculous. You're still a Bourke and you're still my brother, and I'm still head of the clan. I want you to tell me what it is you know. I'm tired of you keeping secrets and skulking around. All you're doing is putting the rest of us in a bad position by keeping things to yourself. Don't play the hero, telling yourself you're only doing it for my good. Because I'm not going to stop trying to help you."

"You should. You shouldn't be here." He glanced up at the sky, breathing hard.

"Too late. Now tell me."

He waited a long time, but I would always outwait him when it came to getting what I wanted. "I'm not here to get protection from Lucian," he finally admitted.

"Why are you, then?"

He peered over his shoulder at me. "I'm here to kill him."

I gasped, throwing my hands over my mouth. "Do you know what you're saying?" I hissed when I was finally able to speak again.

"Yes, I do."

"You're honestly telling me you're here to kill the head of the North American vampires? The most powerful vampire we know? The head of the League of Vampires? You're going to kill him?" I was barely whispering, barely moving my mouth. No wonder he'd wanted to get so far away from headquarters before speaking with me.

"Yes. That's what I'm telling you."

"But why? I don't understand." I wrapped my arms around myself, suddenly much colder than the breeze sweeping over me. I felt alone in the middle of the barren trees, even with my brother there with me.

"No, you don't, and that's why it would be better if you didn't know."

"No way. You don't get to do that." I walked around him, looking up into his face. "And stop turning away from me. I need to know now. You can't say something like that and not explain why. I need to know you haven't lost your mind, Gage."

"I haven't. I'm saner than I've ever been in my life."

"So why, then? Why?"

"Because he set the Great Fire and blamed our parents."

I took a step back. Would there ever be an end to the horror he was sharing with me? If this was what being clan leader was all about, he could have it. I didn't want it.

"No," I whispered. My mind refused to believe it. I couldn't entertain the idea of Lucian doing something like that to anybody, but especially not to my parents.

He nodded, a grim smile on his face. "That's how I felt when I first found out. I remember how horrified I was. I was sure he would never do anything like that. Not Lucian. Everybody loves and respects him, right?"

"Right."

"It's an act." His smile turned into a sneer. "He's evil, wicked. A liar. He uses others and manipulates them."

"But why our parents?"

"I don't know," he admitted. "I only know they're gone because of what he did. When it became clear he had framed them, they ran. They had to, don't you see? It was the safest thing for us, the kids."

"Did he kill them?" I whispered, and tears sprang to my eyes when I thought about them.

My handsome father. My beautiful mother. I hadn't seen them in decades. One day, they were gone. No explanation. No goodbyes.

"I don't know. Who knows what really happened?"

"But there's a chance they're alive, and they ran because of the fire? To protect us?" I couldn't help hoping.

"Like I said, there's no way of telling... but that's not the point. The point is, it was Lucian, and it was a deliberate move. And I know he slaughtered my guys, too, or sent the ones who did. He's behind everything, don't you get it? He holds all the strings and controls us all like puppets." He slammed his fist into his palm again and again. "I have to do something. I need him dead."

"No, Gage. You must have the wrong information."

Not only did I not want to believe Lucian—Vance's father—could have done it, but I didn't want to encourage Gage on what was nothing more than a suicide mission. There was no way he could get close to the great vampire, not with the way he protected himself. Lucian could see three steps ahead, everybody said. I didn't know if he could read minds or what, but he always foresaw danger and took steps to prevent it from touching him.

"I have the right information. Don't worry."

"How? How did you find out?"

"No. You don't get to know that. The less you know, the better—I've already told you too much as it is." He turned away, shaking his head.

He paced the perimeter of the little clearing we'd stopped in. The crisscrossing branches overhead allowed in a little bit of starlight here and there. The sky was still deep black, which told me I had plenty of time before dawn. But how long would it take to convince my brother he was wrong and should come home with me, or at least give up his crazy plans?

"I can't have you doing this," I whispered. There was a plea in my voice, desperation. I couldn't let him take his life in his hands. "Please, Gage. Tell me you'll give this up and come with me. I'll protect you."

"Nobody can protect me." He stopped pacing and glared at me from across the clearing. "The entire reason I came to him for help was to convince him I didn't know he was behind it. I want him to think I trust him. If he does, he won't suspect me. Get it?"

"I get it. You don't have to explain. But that doesn't make it a good idea." I ran my hands through my hair, my mind racing. What could I say to get him to give it up? I couldn't let him get himself killed over some crazy theory, which was basically all he had to share with me up to this point. A theory. There was no proof. There couldn't be. Not Lucian. Not Vance's father.

"I never said you had to help me," he muttered.

I had never felt so helpless in my life. It was like standing back to watch somebody willfully kill himself. He wouldn't listen to a word I had to say.

He stared at the ground. "How's Jonah?" he asked in a quiet, almost soft, voice.

"I don't know. He's gone."

"Gone?" He looked up at me, questions in his eyes.

I nodded. "He went away. With the half-breed."

He nodded. "That's good for him. Probably better he's not part of this." He walked to me, took my hands in his. "I need you."

"Me? For what?"

"To join me in the war against Lucian."

"No."

"Clan versus clan. We have the power. We have the bodies. We're strong. We can band together."

"No, I said. It's suicide. Don't you get it?" I could tell from the half-crazed appearance in his eyes he didn't.

It was too late to get him to listen to reason.

❧ 22 ❧

JONAH

"What is this place?" I glanced around. The light coming through the open door revealed a little more about the structure of the walls and floor. It was like a tomb. I shivered as I remembered the tombs all around me when I first saw my father again.

No, not my father. I couldn't think of him that way. He was Fane. I had to think of him as Fane.

I couldn't run the risk of telling anyone I'd met my father again. If I let anything slip, which I didn't plan to but it was still possible, I could only refer to him as Fane. I had to get in the habit.

Fane. Fane. Fane. I repeated it in my head as if it were a mantra.

"It's somewhere far away from where you were." Marianelle was very good at answering questions without actually answering them. She knew precisely the words to use.

What would Fane do? I told myself to stop thinking about him—I didn't want anyone there to know I had been with him, not even Anissa, not when he told me how dangerous it was to be near him or know he was alive. No matter how I tried, though, I couldn't help but remember what it was like to stand in his presence again. It had been so long. Knowing he was still alive should have been a gift, and it was a gift—one that came with a heavy price, however.

Would he go after Gage? I should've asked him where to find Gage. I should've asked what Lucian had to do with any of what had happened. Why was he a threat to Gage or any of us? Maybe I should've gone with him. I should've stayed there.

No. I couldn't have. Whenever I looked at or touched Anissa and saw the way she stared up at me with so much trust and faith, I knew I couldn't have gone. Not if it meant being away from her, not knowing where she was or whether or not she was safe. And there wouldn't have been any way to let her know where I was, either, or what I was doing. She would wonder why I had left her. Talk about an unbearable situation. It would've torn me apart— and that wasn't the optimal mindset to be in when I was trying to help my brother. If he deserved my help.

She was shaking. I touched her shoulder and felt her trembling under my hand. "You're a mess."

"Tell me something I don't know," she whispered, laughing shakily.

"Here. Let me." I picked the refuse from her hair—the grime turned her almost white hair to a dull brown—before brushing off her clothes. She had been underground, for sure. There was muck caked in the creases of her neck, the creases of her pants. Inside the tops of her boots—I helped her take them off to shake them out before putting them back on. She turned her pockets out and more dirt shook free.

"What happened to you?" I asked.

Her cheeks reddened. "I need to get cleaned up, for sure."

"You still look good to me," I murmured as I ran a hand over her filthy, dusty hair.

Even caked with dirt as she was, she seemed to glow with a sort of incandescence. I couldn't keep from staring at her, the way a moth was drawn to a flame. She was my flame. I had to protect her.

"Even so, I would feel much better if I were cleaner," she

murmured. Her eyes were wide, reminding me of a rabbit in a trap. Like she didn't know what to expect next.

Neither did I.

"I understand that." There was also my need to be alone with her. Was there anywhere we could be truly alone—especially since she was, in essence, a flight risk? Would Steward take the chance of leaving us on our own again?

I noticed how cold he was toward Marianelle, and how much she seemed to revel in the way he looked at her. She was toying with him. I wasn't sure I wanted to know what was going on between the two of them. Regardless of what it was, he seemed a little distracted.

And Allonic—well, I didn't know the story with him. Only that he seemed to hover around Anissa. I would have to keep an eye on him. What were his real intentions? It was clear Anissa and I had a lot of catching up to do, even after spending what was really a short amount of time apart.

I especially wanted to tell her what happened on the other side of the portal. No, I couldn't tell her the specific details. Only that I had met the infamous Fane. She would know who he was. Everyone did. I would tell her Fane knew where my brother was, but that I hadn't had the chance to get the information from him before he transported me back to where I'd come from.

It didn't matter what I wanted to tell her if we never made it back to somewhere we could be alone. I felt the presence of the others very acutely. Marianelle managed to pry her eyes from Steward long enough to shoot me a knowing look. She was the only one who knew exactly where I had been and exactly who I'd been with.

Or was she?

Allonic seemed to be giving me a knowing look, too. Almost like he knew exactly what was happening inside my head, or at least like he could get a feel for it. How was that possible? Could he feel all others, not just his sister? What an unnerving thought.

I turned to the witch. "How can I get a hold of you when I need to return?"

"Return where?" she asked. "Or should I say, to whom?"

"Enough of your games. We both know he wouldn't be happy if he knew you were playing them with me."

Anissa's hand slid into mine. "We all know who you're talking about."

"You do?" My head snapped around in her direction.

She nodded. "Yes. Allonic told us that was where you were going—to meet with Fane." She squeezed my hand, but I could hardly feel it. There was too much going on inside to process minute by minute.

"At any rate," I managed to sputter, wondering how much danger Anissa was in by knowing who I'd been with. "How do I find you?"

I noticed Anissa glaring at Marianelle when I spoke to her. I could feel a seething anger rolling off her in waves, and her pulse raced. I felt it in her wrist, pressed against mine. She was upset—beyond upset. I peered down at her, and she shot a pointed look up at me.

"I'll explain later," I whispered. "Don't get ahead of yourself."

I heard a rushing noise as I finished speaking, and when I squinted again at the space Marianelle had just occupied, it was empty. Only a tiny, fading dot of light remained. She'd thrown a portal and vanished into it without a word.

"Damn!" I growled, exhaling in frustration.

What was I supposed to do then? She was the only one who could lead me to him. I couldn't run the risk he would summon me again, especially when I'd made it clear I had no desire to look for my brother. It didn't mean I didn't want to see him again, however. I couldn't trust he would understand what was happening in my heart.

Anissa frowned. It was clear she didn't know why I was so desperate for Marianelle's help. She apparently took me the wrong way, down to withdrawing her hand from mine. Terrific.

Something else I had to deal with. Why not? I didn't have enough going on.

I turned to Steward, who seemed more himself once out of the presence of the witch. There was an almost tangible chemistry between them—not a very sweet one, but it was palpable nonetheless. "What do we do now? Go back to the Sanctuary?"

He shook his head. "It's not safe there anymore. I'm not entirely sure how safe it is for me." His deep voice was heavy with concern.

I felt a stabbing pang of guilt. I had put him in danger, when all he'd ever tried to do was help me.

"I'm sorry." Although, I knew as the phrase left my lips how inadequate my words were.

"I understand. Now, it's just a matter of finding somewhere else to send you."

Allonic stepped in. "I might be able to find a place."

"You could?" Anissa asked.

I heard so much hope in her voice, my heart went out to her. Something had passed between them while I was gone.

He nodded. "I need a little time."

Her face fell. "Time? I don't think we have time. I don't think we can afford to waste another minute." She took a few steps away from me then started pacing back and forth, arms crossed over her abdomen. She muttered something under her breath, as though debating whether or not to do something. I only wished I knew what was happening in her head. I looked at the others and could tell they were just as confused as I was.

"All right." She finally turned to us. "I think I know where we can go. It's the safest place right now, all things considered."

"And where would that be?" Allonic asked.

She only gave him a cryptic smile.

That smile didn't give me a very good feeling.

I didn't like the idea. In fact, I sort of hated the idea. But once I weighed our options, I knew it was the only answer.

I turned to Steward and Allonic. Both of them were waiting for me to say something. I wondered how it was possible for two beings to be so alike, yet so different. Then again, it was the same for any creature. My sister and I were both vampires, yet we were very different. Same thing with me and Jonah. We were alike—very alike in many ways—but fundamentally different. Maybe it was their similarities that put them at odds with each other. They were so similar, they rubbed up against each other.

That whack to the back of Steward's head probably hadn't helped things, either.

I took a deep breath. They wouldn't like what I was about to say. "I need you to take us to league headquarters."

I had expected one or both of them to protest, but Jonah spoke before they had the chance. "Absolutely not!"

I glanced at him. "Why not?"

"Because it's the worst idea I've ever heard. I mean, we just came from there. We were thrown out—well, you were thrown out. I left on my own. Still, I don't think they'll roll out a red carpet for us." His brow creased when he frowned. "I can't imagine why you would want to go back there."

"It's the only place we can go where there's a remote chance of safety," I said. "The League of Vampires won't turn you away."

"And you? You're—"

"I know what I am." I nodded. "And this is still the best idea. I need you to trust me right now."

"You've said that before. Look where it got us." He glanced around the room, then back at me with a cocked eyebrow.

"Point taken," I murmured, blushing again. "Still, this is right. I mean it. Please."

He thought it over then sighed.

I knew I would hear that sigh. It meant he was about to give in to me.

"Are you sure about this?" Steward asked.

"Do you have any other ideas?" I faced Allonic. "I'm sorry— not that I don't want your help, but we need to move fast."

"I understand."

Steward spoke again. "All right. If you're sure about this, I can take you to the meadow not far from the Sanctuary—but that's as far as I can go."

It was better than nothing. I looked at Jonah, who shrugged. "I don't think I have much of a say right now. This is all your plan."

My nose wrinkled. "You might as well tell me it's my funeral."

He chuckled as he took my hand.

We were in it together, and that was all I needed to know. I hoped my plan worked.

Allonic held up a hand. "Here." He removed his cloak, revealing a simple tunic and pants beneath it. "You'll need this."

"Why?" Still, I reached for it. I could almost feel power tingling in the fabric. I wondered what its purpose was, then I remembered the way he'd covered me with it when we traveled to the room we were in now.

"You'll need it if you don't want the company of a spiritwalker."

I knew Allonic was thinking about how I'd fought off the wraith Steward had sent into me.

"Why would we need one, anyway?" Jonah asked.

"They're necessary for you to pass through a shade portal," he explained.

"Why couldn't you have told us that to begin with?" Jonah was clearly incensed.

I shared the sentiment.

"It's easier for you not to know when time is of the essence," Steward explained then glared at Allonic.

I could feel the tension between them rising again.

"Time is of the essence now," I reminded them.

"Share it with Jonah," Allonic advised. "That way, you'll both be able to pass through."

"Thank you," Jonah replied.

It was nice to see them getting along together—we may have just met, but Allonic was still my brother. If the two of them got along, so much the better.

"Wait a minute. If we need a cloak to get through a shade portal, how come we could walk in and out of Sanctuary without a cloak or spiritwalker?"

He smiled indulgently, like someone speaking to a child. "The way you got in and out Sanctuary? That's not a portal. It's only a hidden entrance. Before Jonah showed it to you, you never would have found it. Once someone does show it, it's like a key of sorts. Now you know it's there. You can't miss it, can you?"

"No. And it's hard to believe I ever would have overlooked it before."

He nodded. "That's how it works. The entrance you used opens directly to Steward's quarters. It's his personal one."

"Excuse me," Steward said.

We both looked at him. He was glaring at my brother. "Are

you sure you aren't sharing too much information? It's one thing to share your cloak..."

Allonic drew himself up to an even taller height.

I could feel the animosity building all over again. It was enough to make me roll my eyes.

"There's nothing wrong with sharing information... and my cloak with my sister," he said in a dangerous tone of voice. "My mother would want me to help her, don't you think?"

Steward didn't look impressed. "Your mother is not a shade or a memory keeper. She has no responsibilities or accountability to the shades, unlike you or me. It doesn't matter if she wants you to help your sister or not. She doesn't live by our rules."

Allonic laughed. "That's funny, coming from you. You're the one who brought the vampires in. You're the one who showed them the entrance in the first place." He pointed to Jonah, who looked less than pleased to be dragged into their fight. "You might as well have given them the key to the Sanctuary, since they can get right in thanks to you telling them how to. Don't chastise me about what I should and shouldn't do. You have no right."

Steward opened his mouth to reply, but I beat him to it. "Speaking of. I want to see my mother."

"Anissa, I wanted to talk to her first."

"So, what are you saying?" I asked, shocked and hurt. "That she wouldn't want to see me? You had to clear it with her first?" My heart ached unspeakably, even more than when I found out she was still alive and hadn't reached out to me. She didn't want me at all. The sketches didn't mean anything if she didn't want to take the chance and be with me.

I could hardly process everything I was feeling. It was like information overload. There was so much spinning through my head, nothing got through. I was numb. I almost didn't feel Jonah's hand touch my arm.

"We should go, quickly."

I nodded. He was right. I would let Jonah take care of things for a little while. In the meantime, I would get my head straightened out. And my heart.

I spread the cloak between my two outstretched arms, and Jonah took one end to wrap around himself. Only when we were both covered did Steward lead us through the portal, back to the meadow just outside the Sanctuary.

Allonic followed.

Moments later, we were outside again. It was still dark, the moon ripe and bright.

"Thank you," I whispered to Allonic as I handed back his cloak. "You know how much that meant to me."

"I do." He fastened it again at his throat.

I couldn't help asking, my curiosity getting the best of me even as my heart ached. "How does it work? Why did it make it possible for us to get through the portal?"

He touched the rough, strong cloth. "It's imbued with the essence of spiritwalkers. That's how it makes crossing through shade portals possible. The only way non-shades can go through."

I knew we needed to leave—we were out in the open, at the mercy of any Enforcer that might come along. Still, I couldn't help but mention it again. "One day, I want to see my mother. I need to."

"And I'm sure she'll insist on it. I didn't want you to think she wouldn't want to see you. It's not like that at all. She wants to see you. And Sara."

"She does?"

"As long as you don't hate her. I think that's what she's most afraid of."

My breath caught in my throat. "I could never hate her," I whispered. "Not ever."

"She'll be glad to hear that." He smiled.

"How... how will I find you?" I asked, though I felt Jonah's eagerness to get out of here and knew time was ticking away. We still had to course to headquarters, which would take time. We had to get to safety before dawn.

"I'm a shade, remember? I'll find you."

I reached for him, and he took my hand. Something unspoken passed between us.

"You have to hurry," Steward said, regret in his voice. "You're in danger. I'm sure there are Enforcers who will want to find the Enforcer you killed."

"You killed an Enforcer?" Jonah asked, mouth hanging open.

"There's a lot we need to catch up on," I told him. "I did. And I fed on him. And you need to tell me about Fane."

Steward cleared his throat. "I'm sure there are shades searching for you, too," he added, as though we needed more of a reason to get out of here.

"Thank you," I whispered to him then looked at my brother one more time.

I hoped he was right, that he could find me when he wanted to. I needed to see my mother. Knowing she was there somewhere, filled me with conflicting emotion. I wanted more than anything to feel her arms around me again. I wanted to rest my head on her shoulder and let go of everything I'd been carrying around for so long. Everything Marcus made me do, everything I went through after saving Sara. All of it. Only my mother could help me make sense of it.

I took Jonah's hand and rested easy in the knowledge that at least I wouldn't have to think about anything while we coursed. He would lead the way. Good thing, too—I was so numb, so emotionally spent, I wished I were human. At least humans could sleep.

❧ 24 ❧

PHILIPPA

I left Gage in the basement, where I'd found him. There was no helping him, and the more I tried, the more hopeless I felt. It was like trying to get through quicksand. The more I fought, the more it sucked me in.

"I'll get back to you later," I murmured before leaving him.

He nodded, and there was still a hopeful light in his eye.

I hated to see it. He had to know I couldn't join him. I couldn't give my blessing to a war. How had things fallen apart so quickly?

Vance waited at a distance.

I could hardly look at him.

His father. Had his father started the Great Fire? Had he blamed my parents? Was he the reason they went away? I couldn't bring myself to believe it, especially when I saw the sincerity in Vance's eyes. It was more than I could stand.

"What's wrong?" he asked when I reached him.

"Who says there's anything wrong?"

"Sure. Act like I don't know you."

I rolled my eyes. "Why does there have to be anything wrong? I talked to my brother. It shook me up a little. What do you expect?"

He nodded thoughtfully. "I guess that makes sense. Is he all right?"

"I wouldn't say that," I replied, trying to sound light. "I wouldn't say that at all."

He cupped my face. "I hate seeing you so worried," he whispered. "I hate him for doing this to you. I'm sorry, but it's true."

I closed my hands over his. "I appreciate that, but it's my problem to deal with, not yours. Don't worry yourself too much about it."

I wished he wouldn't touch me this way—not that I didn't like it, but because I liked it way too much. It was so hard to keep my heart under wraps when he made me feel the way he did.

He wouldn't let go, though I tried to pull away.

"Have dinner with me," he murmured, gazing into my eyes.

I almost melted into him. How could I help it?

"Where?" I asked.

"Nearby." He smiled, taking my hand in his. "Come on. I'll show you."

In a flash, I was in his arms—he was too fast for me to protest —and before I could blink an eye, we were coursing to the top of one of the spires on either side of the cathedral's body. I didn't have time to think or process what was happening before we reached the top.

"Wow," I gasped when he set me on my feet. "You don't let a girl get a word in edgewise, do you?"

"I find it's harder for a girl to fight me when I don't give her the chance." He grinned.

"That's very reassuring." I surveyed our surroundings—we were at the top of the world, or so it seemed.

For miles in all directions, all I saw were trees and rolling hills. The sky was clear, the moon shining luminously. It was a beautiful night, and I was in the middle of it. Almost touching the stars.

I could hardly believe what was waiting for me up there. A table, set up with a tablecloth, lit candles, and two crystal goblets. In each goblet was a healthy pour of rich, dark-red blood.

"You set this up in advance?" I asked.

"I had to do something while you were off with your brother" He shrugged.

I didn't want to ask him how he'd suddenly become so resourceful. It was better not to know. It would break the spell he was weaving around us.

No. I couldn't give into the spell. That was what he wanted me to do, but it would only hurt me.

"I'm not here for romance, you know," I reminded him. "I hate to think of you wasting your time trying to woo me like this."

"Woo you? Me?" He shook his head. "I don't know what you're talking about."

"So you set up romantic scenarios like this for everybody?"

"Maybe I do."

"Well, you can stop wasting your time, like I said. The past is long over."

"We were young then." He shrugged. "I made mistakes."

"Young is a pretty relative term when you're a vampire, isn't it? In many ways, we haven't aged at all."

"Very funny."

"I mean it, though. And my heart hasn't aged. It hasn't moved on, even though you want it to." I shrugged. "I'm sorry, but that's how it is."

And I wished it wasn't because, as fresh as the hurt still was, I also remembered how deeply I had cared for him. I still felt tied to him, even though I wanted anything but that. I didn't want us to have any ties at all. I wanted to be able to move on.

I should've been happy with somebody like Sledge, for instance. I couldn't help thinking about him as I sat at the table—no sense in letting a feast like this go to waste, was there?

No, I wasn't crazy about Sledge acting so possessive, but I'd had fun on our dates. A lot of fun. He wasn't charming or sexy the way Vance was, at least not in the same way. But there was a freshness about him, a realness Vance couldn't touch. He was a "what you see is what you get" sort, and I appreciated that. When he told me something, I could believe he meant it. If he ever promised to be faithful to me, he would be faithful. I'd never have to worry.

One night, we'd sat up on the roof—simply talking. I'd told him all about missing my parents, and how much it hurt me when I knew about Gage's resentment of Jonah's leadership. He had understood. He hadn't cut me off to talk about himself. He'd listened, really listened, absorbing my words instead of only nodding and waiting for his turn to talk.

And when he had spoken, it was like he understood me. I didn't have to overexplain. He knew how I felt.

If only he wasn't such a bonehead about so many other things. Like giving me space when I needed it and not treating me like a possession of his.

When Vance sat down, I asked, "Why are you moving to New York? Aren't your father's headquarters in Chicago?" They had been for decades, maybe a century or more. I knew Lucian had started out on the East Coast, like my family, but had moved on at the turn of the twentieth century.

"Yeah, but I have a couple of projects out here that are taking up my time," he said.

He didn't elaborate, so I decided to let it go.

"How are things going with your father, by the way?" Yes, I was trying to get information about Lucian. I couldn't forget what Gage had said.

"All right, I guess." He shrugged then turned his attention to the blood in his goblet.

"He looked well at the meeting."

"Yes, he did. He's been very well lately."

"I wanted to have the time to say hello to him, but I didn't, obviously. I hope he understood it was all the confusion going on and not a slight against him."

"Oh, I'm sure he understood. He's pretty smart, you know."

Yes, very smart. Very clever. "As long as he doesn't think I meant it against him."

"He doesn't. I'm sure of it. He was impressed by the way you stood up and took control of the clan," he offered.

I smiled as I raised the goblet to my lips. Impressed, was he? Yes, and he looked very pleased. He was very quick to approve my leadership, wasn't he? I couldn't help but view things through the lens of Gage's accusations. I wished he had never told me the things he had.

I couldn't get any more from him, no matter how I tried. He didn't seem very interested in his father's work, but that was nothing new. He had never been one to pay attention to the ins and outs of his father's business, much less his political interests as head of the league. He left that up to his siblings. He had always been content to coast along and enjoy life. I wished for once he would be a little more responsible and aware. He wasn't any help to me the way he was.

"Have you heard anything about Jonah?" he asked.

I looked down at the silk tablecloth. "No."

"You don't know where he is?"

"Why are you so curious all of a sudden?"

He shrugged. "I don't know. It seems like as good a question as any. I mean, you found one brother. I was wondering about the other one, is all."

"Your guess is as good as mine." I didn't feel comfortable telling him anything, even if there had been anything to tell. How far could I trust him? How much did he know about his father? He wouldn't share it with me, of course, even if he knew his father's alleged crimes. His allegiance would be to his family.

He didn't seem to think it was strange I wouldn't talk about it. Instead, he turned the topic back to us. "Like I tried to tell you after the meeting, I want to see more of you now that I'm moving to the city."

I shook my head, laughing a little. "I knew you would say that."

"What's wrong with it?"

"Do we really have to go through this again? Why are you being deliberately obtuse?"

"What's that supposed to mean?" He frowned, his handsome face contorting a little when he did. He wasn't used to not getting his way. He expected girls to crumble in front of his charm.

"It means you refuse to acknowledge how much you hurt me. I'm sorry if I'm not jonesing to get hurt again, Vance. Especially when I have so much on my plate at the moment. It's not fair to do this to me."

It was so hard to resist him. It would've been so easy to give in. My heart wanted me to—half of it, anyway. The other half reminded me, loud and clear, how easily he'd broken it before. I couldn't trust him, no matter how much I wanted to.

He looked like he was about to shoot back some clever reply, one eyebrow cocked, when a sound interrupted us.

Footsteps on the stairs.

We turned in the direction of the sound, and my eyes went wide when I made out the shape of a beautiful brunette in a slinky evening gown, the red satin cut low in the front to the point where she was barely covered at all. It was tight, flowing over her body like water.

And she didn't appear happy when she saw me sitting here with Vance.

❧ 25 ❧

PHILIPPA

"You're late," she snarled to Vance, her red lips parting to show white fangs.

Oh, she was furious.

Thick, heavy, dark hair swung over one shoulder as she threw her head back and gazed at him with a sneer.

"I'm busy." His voice was tight, no-nonsense.

I didn't look at him, so I couldn't read his expression. I only had eyes for her. Although I knew it shouldn't, my pulse started racing. I was disappointed another girl had shown up even as Vance had sworn to me it was all in the past. Like I needed proof we were all wrong together.

Good thing I didn't take my eyes from the other vampire because she didn't waste time in lunging at me, claws extended.

I leapt out of my chair and caught her before she knocked me down—she might throw me out of the tower if I wasn't careful. I shoved her back, and she stumbled on her high heels.

"I don't know why you're mad at me, but I have to tell you there's no reason. I don't want to have anything to do with him." I glanced at Vance. "And I mean that right now. But I won't let you attack me without fighting back."

She glared at me. "Have it your way." And she rushed me again, ready to fight.

Good. I needed something to vent my anger on, anyway.

Vance stepped in, stopping her. "What's wrong with you? Why are you acting like this, Adriana? You need to go. Now."

"Don't tell me what to do," she spat. "I can't believe I ever fell for your lines, you no-good, two-timing..." Then she lunged at him, wrapping her fingers around his throat.

He pushed her away, but she went back for him. They knocked over the table, sending the crystal crashing to the stone floor. I hurried to put out the candles before they set the table on fire.

No sense in sticking around to see how things turned out. I used their distraction as a means to slip away unnoticed, coursing down from the tower and all the way back home to New York City before I could second-guess myself.

There was so much happening in my head and my heart, and even the strain of coursing to Manhattan didn't help. I could usually lose myself, clear my head. But it wasn't possible. Not when I felt as badly as I did. Betrayed. Terrified for my brothers—both of them, but especially Gage. Fearful of another war. How could I lead my clan through a war? Would I be a good leader? No, a good leader stopped a war before it ever happened. I couldn't let Gage take things that far. But what other choice did I have when he was so determined?

And Vance. How could he do that to me? Trying to tell me he wanted to see more of me. Yeah, he wanted to see more of a lot of girls, didn't he? The creep. I'd been right about him. It wasn't a good idea to let myself care again. My instincts were always right. I had to learn to value them more, didn't I?

I didn't slow down until I reached the high rise, and I went straight up to the penthouse when I got there. The weakness and weariness from coursing and going through so much in such a short time left me desperate for blood.

I wasted no time going straight to our supply—forget using a glass. I tore the spout from the bottom of the bag and held it to my lips, gulping it straight down. So what? There was nobody there to see me or stop me.

I was alone, in essence. Even Scott was pretty much lost to me, too worried about Sara to care about me or the clan. The empty penthouse was proof of that. Where was he? Not looking for Gage, I was sure. He wouldn't endanger Sara. I couldn't depend on him. I couldn't depend on anyone. I was alone. The weight of everything hanging over me was nearly enough to crush me. I slumped against the kitchen counter as I drank, desperate for it to give me the strength I needed.

The door opened. Before I could stop myself, in walked Sledge. I didn't like being caught acting like an animal, sucking blood straight from a bag, and I especially didn't like that he happened to be the one who caught me. He took in the whole scene—me, the bag, and I saw a knowing look on his face.

"What happened?" he asked.

I finished drinking and tossed the bag aside. "You don't wanna know." I couldn't have described it if I tried. I was too numb and heartsick to go through it all again. "It's been a long night. Let's just leave it at that."

"You look terrible."

"You're a very smooth talker when you put your mind to it, you know?"

He smiled a little as he came to me, and I wondered what he wanted. I hadn't forgotten the way we'd ended things—with him storming off, furious I'd been with Vance although nothing had been going on. What was on his mind?

He reached for me, running his thumb along the corner of my mouth. I saw red on that finger when he pulled it back. Never taking his eyes from mine, he placed the tip of his thumb in his mouth.

"Where did you go?" he asked in an almost mournful voice.

I knew why, too.

He didn't have to say what he was really wondering—where I had been with Vance.

I slumped even more, leaning against the counter for strength. "I went to see Gage, like I said. Remember? That wasn't a lie." Tears prickled behind my eyes, and he went blurry.

He did just what I needed him to do then. He wrapped his arms around me and allowed me to rest my head against his chest.

"And?" he asked.

"And I'm confused." I sighed.

❧ 26 ❧

O nce we were alone, I could tell her about Fane. It was impossible to think of him as some mythical being.

I couldn't stop thinking of him as Dommik, my father. Head of the Bourke clan. What would she think when she knew he and Fane were one and the same? It was mind-blowing. But would I tell her? Or would it be better to keep that to myself, for her sake?

And I still needed to know how she'd ended up so filthy—was it when she killed the Enforcer? Since when did she kill Enforcers? There had to be a good reason for her to feed from a human. She'd broken the pact. I knew she wouldn't take something like that lightly. There had to have been an emergency while I was gone. And I had left her to that.

Well, it couldn't be helped. I was looking for her at the time.

Before any of that could happen, I needed to get us to headquarters. I hoped she knew what she was doing as I led us across the fields, plains and forests we had already crossed while coursing away from headquarters after the meeting.

It seemed like years had passed since then. The moon sank a little lower in the sky every minute, a reminder dawn was coming in a few hours. We had to move swiftly. I didn't know what she would expect us to do once we got there, and we couldn't risk sun exposure.

Once I knew we were getting close to the cathedral—I could see it in the distance—I slowed down a bit to conserve as much of our strength as possible. We reached headquarters with plenty of time to spare.

"I guess we just go up to the door and see what happens? Or did you have some other plan in mind?"

She shook her head. "I couldn't go into specifics back there at the Sanctuary, since I know how many feel about me being half-blood."

It started coming together then. "You want to go to the fae world? To your father?"

In the light of the moon, her eyes shone. She nodded. "It's our only chance," she whispered. "We'll be safe there."

I was dubious, to say the least. What would her fae brethren think of me? We didn't get along famously—putting it mildly. Would she have to go through the same thing on my behalf?

"You don't think this is a good idea," she murmured, even as she led me to the spot where I'd taken her away from her father.

I hadn't taken her away from her father. No, she'd decided against going with him for my sake. It was her choice. Somehow, I didn't think her father would remember it that way.

"I can't say it's my favorite plan ever," I admitted. "I'm sorry to say it."

"Well, sometimes we have to do what we don't feel comfortable with when it means ensuring our safety." She looked at me from her place a few steps ahead. "You're not afraid of the fae, are you?"

"Who, me?" Not afraid, per se, but I certainly didn't trust them. They weren't exactly adored by other creatures, and it wasn't by accident they'd chosen their own dimension in which to live. Nobody else would have them, I guessed, no matter how valuable their blood.

We approached the same split-trunk tree by which we'd stood

during the league meeting. It was like déjà vu.

"Are you sure?" I asked.

"I'm sure they'll accept you," she muttered, as though reading my mind.

I didn't need to explain to her how apprehensive I was. I looked up at the portal, which I could just make out in between the split halves of the tree trunk.

"All right," I muttered. "Let's get it over with."

"You first," she said, pushing me ahead of her.

"You're kidding." But I allowed her to push me.

There it was, shimmering a few inches beyond my reach. I took one more step toward it and stretched out my hand, intending to test it. I expected to glide through it as I had the one Fane threw. I might as well have tried to pass through a pane of glass.

"I don't understand," Anissa said as I tried again.

No go.

No part of me would pass through.

"It's because I'm not one of the fae," I said. "That's why you can go through and I can't."

"Exactly." We heard the voice before we saw the figure of a woman passing through from the other side into our world.

No, not a woman. She was one of the fae. Her hair shimmered like silver in the light of the moon and hung down her back in a waterfall. She was almost blindingly beautiful.

"Felicity!" Anissa smiled in relief. "I'm so glad to see you."

"I'm glad to see you're unharmed," Felicity replied in a measured voice, devoid of emotion.

I could tell she was weighing her words carefully. So Gregor was still furious with us. I was sure everyone in the fae world had heard about how Anissa had refused him—he struck me as a proud creature. And I doubted he would be happy to learn we had returned.

Anissa didn't seem to care. I had to give her credit for that.

"I need to bring Jonah through with me," she insisted.

"You know he can't enter Avellane without being granted permission." At least Felicity's voice was gentle, even if it was clear she felt we were treading on thin ice.

Anissa didn't seem to notice, or she still didn't care. I couldn't decide which it was.

"Can you grant it? Please. We need to get through. We're in trouble, and we need protection."

Felicity's smile was sad. "I'm aware of that. We all are."

"You are?"

"Yes, and I'm sorry to tell you I'm simply not allowed to grant permission. I don't have authorization."

"Who does?" Anissa asked.

I squeezed her hand. It was obvious, wasn't it?

"I'll ask if he'll grant it to you," Felicity replied. "Wait here. I won't be long." She stepped back through the portal, leaving us alone.

I turned to Anissa. "She's going to your father," I muttered, stroking her face with the backs of my fingers.

It was very possible he wouldn't grant me permission to go through, and I was willing to accept that as long as it meant she was safe. I would find something to do with myself—I might be able to get into league headquarters. She was the one I was worried about being allowed in. Funny how we were both in the same situation.

"What if he says no?" she whispered. "I didn't think about that."

"I know you didn't. I didn't, either, or I wouldn't have tried to get through." I took a deep breath. We were finally alone. "I'm so glad you're all right," I whispered. There was so much I wanted to say to her, but that was the one thought that kept resounding through my head. I was so relieved to be touching her.

"I know the feeling." She grinned. "I was so afraid for you."

I bent to kiss her, but, in the heartbeat before our lips touched, there was movement from the portal. It wasn't Felicity who stepped through.

"Father!"

I stepped back as if Anissa had burned my skin. No way I was going to let Gregor catch me kissing his daughter. I got the feeling I wouldn't have to worry about where to hide out, since he would make short work of me. The dark, murderous expression on his face told me as much.

For all her worry—and I could feel it in her elevated pulse—she looked happy to see him.

I was glad, too, knowing his presence meant she would be safe.

I remembered his last words to us.

Sign your death warrants. I'm disappointed in you both.

He was still disappointed, obviously.

"Why are you here?" he asked.

"We need your help," Anissa explained, breathless.

"Oh. Now you need my help? You didn't need me before, when I warned you how dangerous it would be. Didn't I tell you?"

"Yes, you did. And I'm sorry. Really, I am."

I had the feeling I was taking my life in my hands, but I took the chance. "There's a lot of trouble out here," I confided. "More than even Anissa knows about."

"What?" She looked at me with a frown.

"I'm sorry. I didn't get the chance to tell you before now. We were never alone."

"It's temporary," she told him. "We need safety for a little while, until we decide our next move."

"Are you in trouble?" He glanced around.

"Not in trouble, per se. More like in limbo. There's nowhere safe for us. It seems like no matter where I go, somebody wants my blood."

In limbo. Talk about an understatement.

"And I can't get her to stay still long enough to make sure she's safe," I added.

"Could you please?" she whispered.

Gregor only nodded. "It isn't easy to keep her in one place."

She had run away from him once, after all.

I saw the resolve in Gregor's face. He couldn't abandon his child any more than Fane could abandon Gage. And he would do anything he could to protect Anissa, like Fane would do anything to help Gage—including summoning me to himself, risking the both of us by doing so. Although Gage had betrayed me and his clan, the clan my father used to lead, Fane couldn't write him off —any more than I could. Yes, I finally admitted to myself, I needed to take care of my brother.

What about his betrayal? I asked myself as Anissa and Gregor stepped aside to have a conversation.

What about the way he tried to split up the clan? He undermined me. He went behind my back—not only the back of his leader, but his brother. How could he do that to me?

I remembered the early days, after Mom and Dad disappeared. When it was clear I would be head of the clan, since I was older. He was so bitter in those days, and he didn't bother trying to hide his feelings. Stupid me, trying to tell myself he'd gotten over it. It was clear he hadn't. I should've been honest with myself from the beginning instead of hoping he'd eventually come around and work as a true teammate, the way Philippa always had. She'd always been my advisor. We'd worked together. Gage was my twin. He was the one who should've been my partner. It wasn't meant to be.

And he'd split us up, damn him. He'd tried to take my leadership. Could I risk myself for his sake after he'd done that? I'd already saved him once, when Marcus took him prisoner. Could I do it again? Was it worth it?

I started to turn my attention to what Anissa and Gregor were talking about—their whispers had become a little too loud to go unheard.

Anissa was gesturing wildly, trying to convince her father to take me. I wanted to tell her to stop wasting her time, but the searing pain in my forearm stole the words from my mouth.

A cry of pain bubbled up in my throat, one which I barely

managed to stifle. I inhaled sharply, trying to breathe through the pain. What was happening? It seemed to radiate from the inside.

I told myself to pay attention to Anissa until the pain passed, which it surely would. But there was no way. The pain was searing, blinding, stealing my concentration.

I glanced down at the inside of my forearm to find a raised brand on my skin. It was as if a design had been burned into my skin with a cattle branding iron.

My eyes widened in surprise. It was roughly the size of a half-dollar, full of symbols I didn't recognize. What did it mean? Where had it come from? A brand? Who would brand me? No wonder it hurt so much.

This wasn't good. It was very bad. The sort of bad that could put us both in danger.

What a surprise, I thought dryly. *More danger*. I had barely caught my breath before more threats knocked at my door.

It took all the self-control I possessed to turn my arm inward, hiding the brand. I told myself to stop thinking about the markings and to concentrate on what was happening with Anissa.

She hissed angrily at her father—her voice was low, but I couldn't miss the anger in her words.

"Only you can enter," Gregor said.

Of course, he would.

I couldn't blame him. He would only be inviting danger into his closely-guarded realm if he allowed me entry. I didn't hold it against him. His daughter was another story.

"Then neither of us shall," she shot back. "We'll figure it out somehow. I don't want you to put yourself out on my account." I heard the pain in her voice, the betrayal. I hated thinking I had put her in this position, but that was the truth of it.

The next thought that came to my mind was the position this brand would put her in. I didn't know what sort of dangers it heralded. I couldn't risk having her around if things got ugly. I couldn't have her hurt. I had to do anything and everything to keep her safe.

I took a step in their direction. "No. There's been a change of plans." I moved closer, ignoring Gregor for the moment. I knew he was doing what he thought was best, but I didn't have to be friends with him.

Anissa gasped. Her anger and confusion were palpable. "Excuse me, but why don't I get a say in this?"

I looked at Gregor again. "I might have a few things to take care of, and I don't want her to be part of it, for her own good."

Anissa was fuming. Her arms were crossed over her chest, her demeanor unapproachable.

I turned to her for a moment. "I'm sorry, but I think I might need to take care of the situation with Gage. And I can't let you be part of that. I know it doesn't sound right, but believe me. I would feel much better if I knew you were safe in Avellane with your father."

The murderous expression I'd seen at first had softened into one of concern for his daughter.

"Why can't you come, too?" Her eyes searched my face, pleading.

"Like I said, I think I need to stay behind. But it won't be forever, and I'll get word to you."

"No. I don't like this. You at least need to rest after coursing. You need your strength."

I didn't think I had the time to waste on that, but there was no sense in arguing with her. If I could convince Gregor to take her, that would be enough. I glanced at him again. So did she.

"This is for the best. Stay with your father. I'll come find you when the coast is clear."

"Don't do this," she whispered.

The pain in my arm pulsed, throbbed, reminding me of the presence of the brand. Reminding me how crucial it was to ensure her safety, no matter how it hurt her in the moment.

"It's for the best, like I said. I promise. This will all work out."

I had no idea how, but I needed to believe it would. Otherwise, what was the point of everything we'd been through?

27

JONAH

Anissa glanced at me one more time before Gregor led her through the portal. She didn't simply look at me. She practically cast daggers at me.

I gave her a strong, confident smile—or something I hoped passed for one. I couldn't let her know how concerned I was over what would happen once she went through. Where would I go?

I looked behind me, toward the cathedral. Lights burned inside.

No, I couldn't go there, not when I didn't know what the brand on my arm meant. It burned and stung so deeply it almost made it impossible for me to think clearly. I was too busy wishing the pain would go away. I couldn't do my best strategizing when I couldn't think through the haze of burning pain.

I had never heard of a brand like the one on my arm, but I knew things like that didn't happen on their own. Somebody had done this to me. Somebody with magic.

I had to find Fane. He might be able to tell me. But where was he? How could I get answers from him when I didn't know where to look? Damn Marianelle for disappearing before telling me anything of value. She thought she could play little games like that. I could've killed her for it—that's how furious and hopeless I was.

Fane had been keeping an eye on me all along, using the underground Passages. It made sense, then, I might be able to see him, or at least sense him, from high above the world.

And what better place to keep watch for him than at the top of the clan high rise? I hadn't been there since I'd forfeited my spot at the head of the family.

I wondered if Philippa and Scott would be there waiting for me. I actually hoped not, good as it would be to see them. If they were there, I would feel like a liar if I didn't tell them about seeing Fane. They deserved to know. Still, there was danger. I wouldn't betray him, and I wouldn't put them in that position.

With that in mind, I coursed back to the city. The notion of going home helped me push through the weakness I felt from the last coursing session—it was a good thing home wasn't as far from the cathedral as the Sanctuary was. It only took a half-hour, maybe less, for me to reach Manhattan. The lights and bustle were enough to send pain to my chest. I missed being in the center of a vital, vibrant place. I missed going out with my brothers and sister. I missed the way things used to be, back when I thought I had problems.

But now I had Anissa, and she made up for everything else. I wouldn't have traded her for anything. Except I couldn't be with her at the moment. Not until I had everything figured out. Having her pissed for a short time was better than having her in danger.

I used a back entrance, one that was secret, and entered from below ground that had an elevator which could only be accessed by secret code that opened up to a bookcase in my suite. No one knew about it.

The first thing I noticed on entering the building was the quiet. What was happening that it was so quiet? Had everybody gone out? Were they searching for Gage? Odds were, that was exactly what they were doing. Philippa wouldn't let it rest. If he was missing, which he obviously was from the way Fane had made it sound, they'd gone looking for him. It could be a blessing for me if they did, even though I hated the thought of Philippa and Scott getting close to the trouble Gage was in.

Why didn't Fane tell me more about that? I hadn't given him much of a chance, though, had I? Getting back to Anissa had been my priority at the time. I wouldn't have changed that. I only wished I'd taken another moment to get more information.

It took just a minute to get up to the penthouse, and when the door opened, fatigue swept over me. I hadn't felt so exhausted in all my life.

There wasn't any time for that. I could rest when it was over. Whenever that was.

The penthouse was empty, the lights off. I didn't turn on any of them for fear of alerting somebody to my presence. I wasn't sure why, but the thought of letting others know I was here didn't sit well with me.

I only stopped to shower quickly and change my clothes—it felt good to freshen up, even if the water stung when it hit the brand. I was careful with it, avoiding contact as much as I could.

I finished then went to the roof to start looking for Fane.

The night was dark, but dawn was coming soon. I didn't have much time. I concentrated on feeling him, sending out my thoughts so he might see them. I needed to find him. I didn't have time. Desperation colored my thoughts and my decisions, but I realized that might help me. If he knew the situation I was in, how perilous things were all around, he might be more likely to summon me again.

The cool air was good against my skin, especially my arm. He would know who had marked me. I could rely on him.

"Where are you, Fane?" I whispered, looking out across the hundreds and hundreds of buildings with their thousands of lights.

As though answering my question, two figures emerged from the shadows at the other side of the roof. I tensed, going into a fighting stance as I had in the graveyard before Fane made himself known. Was he one of the figures in the shadows? No. They were smaller, slender. I waited for them to make themselves known.

The first, I recognized right away. Her ruby lips curved into a smile while her emerald eyes snapped at me.

"You," I whispered dangerously.

"Oooh, not happy to see me?" She tilted her head to the side. "When I can help you?"

"You disappeared. You deserted me."

"But I'm here now, aren't I? Don't whine."

Meanwhile, the second witch emerged. She was older than Marianelle, and infinitely more poised. She gave the impression of being ancient with her royal bearing, the way she held her head almost defiantly high. While Marianelle's hair was dark brown, this witch's was raven black to match the black outfit she wore.

"You seek him," she said, and there was weight in the last word. Almost as though it should be spelled with a capital letter.

I nodded.

She didn't break eye contact when she spoke. "Go, Marianelle. I will take him to Fane."

Marianelle paused. "You're sure?" A brow rose.

"Yes." The witch smiled at me. "I'm Sirene. I'll take you to him now." She threw a portal.

I prepared myself for the sensation of being sucked through.

In the blink of an eye, I was back in the graveyard. At least I recognized it this time.

Sirene came with me, closing the portal behind her. In front of me was my father.

"Thank you for bringing me back to you," I breathed. "I have so much I need to know. I have so many questions."

"I didn't expect to see you again quite so soon." He smiled. "But it doesn't feel as though this is a pleasant social call."

I shook my head. No, it was anything but. I bared my arm, turning it so the inside was visible. The brand was darker than ever. At least the pain wasn't quite as sharp as it had been—it had lessened to a deep throb.

Sirene gasped. "He's been marked for protection!"

I looked up from my arm at Fane.

He nodded. "Yes. That's what this is."

"Did you do it?" I asked.

I expected him to nod, but he shook his head, instead. "This is beyond my skills. I have no knowledge of how to do this."

"Did you?" I asked Sirene. "You can tell me."

"I would never do something like this without permission." She glanced at Fane, who looked down at her.

I felt a current flowing between them and wondered what it was all about. It didn't make me feel comfortable, seeing my father connecting with someone who wasn't my mother. But my mother was gone, wasn't she? There was so much to adjust to.

"What about the symbols?" Fane asked her. "Can you read them?"

"Will that help?" I asked.

"It might reveal who branded you," he explained. "But only maybe. We'll see."

"May I? I won't hurt you." Sirene reached for my arm, and I stretched it out to her. She took it in gentle hands, hands in which I felt great magic flowing.

I waited while she examined me closely, her face not far from my skin.

Both Fane and I were silent as we watched her.

She shook her head. "This is so strange. It's a language I have not seen in hundreds of years."

So, she was much older than she looked. That wasn't unusual for witches.

"Can you read it, though?" Fane's voice betrayed concern. He was worried for me, my father.

I tried to push my emotion aside. There would be time for that later, as there would be time to rest.

"I'm trying," she said. "From what I can tell, and this is what truly confuses me, it's Valerius. It seems to be his brand."

She looked up at Fane, whose brow furrowed as he frowned.

"Valerius? He hasn't been heard from in centuries," Fane said.

I searched my memory for mention of his name, but nothing came up. He must have been some truly ancient creature for me to have never heard of him. Another reminder of how much I didn't know. Had I ever been confident about what I knew? Why?

"This is a mystery." Sirene released my arm. "I'm sorry I can't be more help." And she sounded sorry, too.

Unlike my distrust for Marianelle, I trusted Sirene's sincerity.

"Do you mind giving me a little privacy with Jonah?" Fane asked.

My pulse raced. What would he tell me? There was so much I wanted to know. Sirene nodded, moving into the mist. It was still pitch dark outside, and, before long, she blended into our surroundings.

He looked at me, eyes burning into mine. "You came back."

"I had to. I had to find you and learn what you plan to do about Gage. And I needed to figure out about this brand."

He smiled, nodding firmly. "I'm glad to have you with me, son." Hearing him call me that brought up so much. My chest felt tight. I could hardly breathe. His son. My father.

"I want to help in any way I can, but I need you to explain something to me, first."

"What can I help you with?" he asked.

"Why would Lucian hurt Gage? You said this had to do with him, but you never told me what."

He nodded sagely. "Yes. Lucian. He's at the root of everything. I hardly know where to begin" He sat on a tombstone then motioned for me to sit as well.

I took a seat across from him on another cold, hard stone, ready to listen.

❦ 28 ❦

JONAH

I watched my father closely as he decided where to begin his story. There was sadness and pain in his eyes when he started to speak.

"It goes back centuries, the history I have with Lucian. All the way back to when I was a human, named Dommik. My family made their home in Europe then, in an area which is now known as Germany, though we called it Prussia. We were happy, poor and happy. But we didn't know any better back then—we knew there were the wealthy, who lived in the towns, but their lives had little to do with ours. We were content with what little we had.

"My father was a farmer. I spent my days and nights working, either in the fields or in the home. We were always building onto our little thatch cottage, since my mother never seemed to stop having babies. It seemed we spent every summer expanding to allow for yet another young life.

"I was the oldest of ten by the time I became a man and had to decide to move on and create a life of my own. I hated the thought of leaving my family, since I'd become so crucial to the success of the farm. But it was time, everyone thought so. I considered purchasing an adjoining parcel of land, so I could at least be nearby.

"That was when I met Lucian. He was human then, too, and we were roughly the same age. Only we were not at the same place in life. I was content where I was. Lucian, on the other hand, would never be satisfied. He had come from what is now part of France, seeking his fortune in other places. Only he hadn't found it yet.

"Lucian's family had been one of merchants, and he was very skilled at doing business. I knew all there was to know about working the land. He had a plan, he said. We would work together.

"It was intriguing. Lucian had a way of convincing those around him to do what he wanted. He managed to fill my head with stories of how wonderful life would be. We would be rich. We would eventually be able to stop working, hiring others to do it for us. If I stayed where I was, I would only know a life of back-breaking work until I died an early death from constant strain.

"I suppose I should thank him for convincing me. He was right.

"His family was wealthy, as merchants generally were in those days, and his father gave us the money to set up our endeavor.

"All went well for the first few years. It was hard work, but it was work I knew. I didn't mind it. I enjoyed it. It made me happy.

"Then, Lucian met a girl.

"He took his time about introducing her to me. He wanted to make sure she shared his feelings before he did so. But he used to tell me about her, on and on. How beautiful she was, how clever and fiery and full of life. He was planning on sharing his life with her.

"I was happy for him, of course. He was my closest friend, the nearest thing I had to a brother while living so far from my family. I wanted to see him happy, settled down. He always seemed dissatisfied, always wanting more. I thought the presence of a wife and family of his own would settle him down. He would have something to work for other than his own glory.

"After months of courting, he announced he wanted us to

meet. He brought her over for Sunday dinner. The entire day was spent in preparation.

"It was all very exciting—at least, for him. I remember watching him in amusement. I had never seen him lose his senses before, which told me how special this girl had to be.

"Then I met her, and I saw for myself.

"The instant my eyes met hers, when Lucian introduced us, I knew I was in love. It hit me like a bolt of lightning. I couldn't have helped it any more than I could help my need to breathe air. She was the most beautiful thing I'd ever seen— creamy skin, deep-red hair, sparkling blue eyes. She was frank and clever and charming, full of life as he'd described her. She always had a ready laugh, too, telling a joke or see the funny side of a situation. I could hardly stand being too close to her, since she made it hard to breathe. I could hardly look at her for too long.

"I didn't want to feel that way. Please, don't misunderstand me. I didn't want to hurt my best friend. I wished she were anybody else. And I tried hard to keep my feelings for her at bay. I avoided her. I told myself to forget her, that Lucian loved her and she loved him. That they'd planned a life together, a life I had nothing to do with. I was a prosperous farmer by then, much more so than I ever would have been had I stayed near my family. I owed that to him. I owed him everything.

"But love can't be helped. And what I didn't know at the time, what I didn't learn for several months, was she'd fallen in love with me, too. It had been the same for her as for me when we met. She'd fought it as I did, or she'd tried to out of loyalty to Lucian.

"It didn't work, needless to say. One day, we crossed paths on the road leading to town. She looked so beautiful that day—more beautiful than I could remember seeing. The crisp morning air put color in her cheeks, and the blue sky somehow made her eyes look more blue. I couldn't help the surge I felt for her in my heart, like she was the entire world. I knew, when she looked straight into my eyes and took my hand as we spoke, she felt the same as I did.

"I can't tell you how conflicted I felt. On one hand, my life was just beginning. She loved me. She had fought it as I had, but it was pointless. She loved me. We were meant to be. I just knew it. I had never loved before, you see, and I understood why that day on the road. I'd been waiting for her.

"On the other hand, the certainty of how crushed Lucian would be as a result was almost enough to shatter my happiness. I hated myself for being so weak. He trusted me, and he loved her. What could we do? I met with her as much as I possibly could, and we would always find ourselves talking about what to say to him. How could we tell him in a way that would lessen the pain? We had to do it, soon, because the more time that passed the worse it would be. We knew that much, though neither of us was exactly eager to get on with it.

"When we did tell him, holding hands to bolster each other, it was like witnessing a house fall. He seemed to crumble in front of us. The pain spread across his face and it felt like I was going through the same pain. I can't tell you the way I recriminated myself for betraying him. I can't say how many times I apologized, either. More than I could count.

"Needless to say, he refused to forgive me. I had considered that, of course. It was his nature—I'd betrayed him, you see. He couldn't get past that. And so, rather than stay and face his heartbreak, he left. He became a mercenary soldier. None of us heard word from him, not even his family. He cut ties completely, either out of embarrassment over being jilted or because he wanted a new start.

"Elena and I were married, of course. You know what happened after that—you and Gage were born, then Philippa, then Scott. Years passed. You began to grow, all of you. I can't tell you how much joy I felt, watching you all learn and love each other. You four reminded me of your mother with your high spirits and fiery tempers.

"I purchased land with the fortune I'd made and turned that into my business. It gave us greater stability. Life couldn't have been better.

"Then, Lucian came back. I'll never forget the day he walked into my office one evening to declare he'd returned.

"Immediately, I saw the change in him. He was pale, drawn, thin. His eyes seemed to glow in a way they never had before. He assured me he had never felt better, too, even when I expressed concern over the change in him. He wouldn't tell me where he'd been or where he was going. I thought, maybe time had softened him. Maybe he'd gotten over what happened and had moved on.

"I didn't know he was a vampire then. I didn't know such things existed—there had been legends, but that was as far as my understanding went. This was centuries ago, of course, and we were less knowledgeable about such things.

"I brought him home to dinner, at his insistence. You were very young, around six years old, so you might not remember that night. He was charming and warm. He took each of you children on his knee and asked you questions and told jokes to make you laugh. I was sure we could go back to the way things were before.

"Then, the following day, he turned your mother to a vampire.

"His plan was to force her to be with him forever. He thought she would leave me and the children, maybe out of shame. It was the only way he could think to win. He'd never stopped loving her, you see, but his love had turned to obsession over the years. And hatred had hardened it. He was determined to take her by any means necessary.

"What he didn't count on was she would tell me what he'd done.

"She didn't run from me. She gave me the choice of joining her, instead. I can't pretend I didn't need to think long and hard about it first—though I loved her more than anything, it meant giving up life as I knew it. But there was no point in existing without her. And so, I agreed. And I've never regretted that choice, as I've never regretted the decision to marry your mother. The happiest years of my life were spent with her, and with you.

"Lucian has never forgiven me for what I did in taking her away and, again, in allowing her to change me. Then I turned you, too, all of you once you were old enough to decide for yourselves if you wanted to join us. We were still a family, which was the last thing he wanted us to be. He hated our happiness. He's never been able to get over it, even after a century and a half."

When Fane's voice trailed off, the silence was nearly deafening. I'd never had the slightest idea. I didn't remember Lucian visiting, either, though it made sense, considering how young I was when he had. No one remembered everything that happened when they were six years old—especially when they'd already lived as long as I.

"And you think he's done something as a result of this?" I asked. "You think he's getting his revenge?"

Fane's mouth twisted into a grim smile. "I think he's been celebrating his revenge for years now."

❦ 29 ❦

I was so pissed, I swear I could almost see red.

I couldn't believe Jonah would leave me like this. After we had damned near broken our necks to get back to each other, he left me with my father and ran away.

Why?

Why?

Why?

"Come." Gregor took me by the arm without waiting for me to reply. I had no choice but to go with him through the portal and into Avellane. On the one hand, it was a relief to leave the uncertainty and worry behind. I didn't have to fear for my safety with my father and his kinsmen—that much I knew for sure. But what good did that do without Jonah?

He must have read the expression on my face, because my father spoke to me before leading me much farther into the settlement.

"It was for the best." His voice was softer than it had been.

That didn't do much to ease the anger I felt toward him. "You could've let Jonah come with us," I grumbled.

"No, I couldn't have."

"Yes, you could have. You have the power to do that. And you could've done it for me." I planted my feet, knowing I was being a stubborn baby but acting like one anyway. I was far too hurt to care very much.

"One day, you'll understand better. Now, let's go." He took my arm again.

I told myself he wasn't dragging me to his home, but that was how it felt.

I sensed gazes on me, eyes looking down from windows carved into the tall, tall trees. They knew why I was here. They had to know I'd already turned my father down when he tried to bring me with him to stay. I ran away. I wondered what they thought of the wayward daughter returning to her fae roots, then told myself it didn't matter very much. They didn't know what I'd gone through. They had no idea how difficult it was for me to swallow my pride and come back when I'd only just refused his protection days earlier.

Yet, no matter how turbulent my thoughts were—and they practically boiled in my brain—my surroundings soon worked their way into my head and heart. I felt my pulse slowing, my fevered thoughts calming as peace crept over me. I would always feel a connection to the trees and lush, almost overgrown grasses and flowers. The sight of the crisscrossing vine bridges far above my head awed me as much as it had when I first saw them. I couldn't shake the feeling I was home, even though I knew I couldn't make it my home if that meant not being with Jonah.

Jonah who had deserted me.

"I've had your chambers freshened up," Gregor informed me in the tone of voice a person used when they were granting a great gift to someone else.

I bit back the snide remark on the tip of my tongue, since the last thing I needed to do was alienate him. He was protecting me, the way a father would. Without him, I'd be out there with nowhere to go, at the mercy of those who wished to do me harm.

"Thank you." I had to choke the words out, but I meant them.

When we stepped into the elevator, or what passed for an

elevator but was more like a cage hoisted by a pulley system made of limbs and vines, the light grew stronger and brighter.

I peered down at my hands to find them unharmed. "It's not sunlight." I remembered the way my skin had burned and blistered the last time I'd been exposed to the rays.

"No, it isn't real sunlight." That was all he would tell me. I supposed he didn't want to reveal all of the fae secrets with me, especially when he didn't know whether or not I would be staying. I could see the sense in that, even if I was growing a little tired of never knowing the full truth of anything.

My chambers were as I remembered them—large, comfortable, and close to my father's. He wanted to keep tabs on me. Well, at least I would have space of my own. The presence of a bed made me smile again. They forgot I didn't need to sleep, though it was good to know I'd be comfortable while resting. I hadn't done that in so long. I needed to regain my strength after coursing. First, there were more important things to address.

There was one very good thing about being here, one thing which picked my mood up instantly: taking a bath. It felt so good to wash away the layers of dirt and blood I'd been carrying on my skin. Like I could wash away the entire, horrible memory. I had killed an Enforcer. I had fed on him, breaking our pact with the humans. What did they think after they found his body lying there in the forest? It galled me that humans did nothing to curb the Enforcers. But that was another matter.

Did they take the news of my actions to the league? I'd done what I had to do—sure, if I hadn't gotten myself into the situation by sneaking around the Sanctuary, I wouldn't have had to do it. I hadn't seen any other option at the moment. I needed Jonah.

And where did it get me? Abandonment. It seemed like we were always saying goodbye, didn't it? Would we ever have a time when it could just be us?

When I left the bath, wrapped in a towel so soft I was sure it was made of magical cloth—and maybe it was, for all I knew— there were clothes waiting for me. So much happened behind-the-scenes, it was a little unnerving. If I stayed there, which I had no intention of doing, I would have to get used to others doing work like that for me. Coming and going while trying not to disturb me.

A knock sounded at the door.

I pulled a long tunic over my head and belted it at my waist before answering. There was a girl outside, and when I first looked at her, I thought she was my sister. That was how much she reminded me of her, the expression on her face.

It wasn't, naturally. I told myself I was thinking of Sara and that made me think the stranger looked like her. Of course, they weren't much alike, not really. The white-blonde hair was the first and major difference.

"Hi," she said, sounding shy.

"Hello."

"Your father told me you were here, and that you might need help with things."

"Such as what?" Why did he always have to stick his nose in? I didn't need a servant, if that was what she was getting at.

"You know, getting around, finding things. He's very busy, of course. He thought you might like a companion or two of your own age." She shrugged a little, smiling.

"You mean you're my bodyguard." I grinned.

"No, he didn't make it sound like that."

Yes, but I knew my father already. He had taken Jonah's mention of my running away to heart. He didn't want to risk losing me again.

"You can come in, if you want." There was more than enough room for two of us and, irritating though it was to have company thrust on me, it was nice not being alone. The girl swept into the room with unspeakable grace. She almost floated over the wood floor, and her long, shining hair rippled when she moved. It was like magic, and she drew my eye to her no matter where she moved. "What's your name?"

"Oh, of course." She held out her hand. "I'm Ardella." Her

smile was bright, shining. She seemed to glow from the inside. Once again, I felt an affinity toward one of my own. I felt like I belonged, even if I was part-vampire. The more time I spent among the fae, the more I understood about myself.

Once I finished dressing, adding a long cloak of sky-blue fabric that shimmered a little in the false sunlight, Ardella and I went for a walk along the bridges connecting the innumerable trees that made up the settlement.

"Do you know how many trees there are?" I asked.

She shook her head. "I don't think there's any way to know. Many, many. More than one creature could count."

"And how many of you are there?"

"Us? You mean, our kind? Your kind?" She gave me a slight smile, and her eyes were understanding.

"I'm sorry." I glanced down, a little embarrassed. "It's not easy, feeling like I belong to two worlds at once."

She looked up and waved at another girl who approached from another bridge, several trees away. We waited for her. I wondered if this was another one of my guards. Why stop at one when I could have two? I held back my opinion. Ardella seemed nice enough, so why make things uncomfortable between us?

"Hello." The second fae greeted me with a benevolent smile and a hug. An actual hug. I didn't know they hugged. She was the warmest of all of the fae I'd met so far. "I'm Marigold. I heard you were here. I didn't get the chance to meet you when you stayed with us before, so I'm glad to have the chance to meet you now."

"You wanted to meet me?" I asked, laughing a little. Ardella laughed, too.

"Who wouldn't?" Marigold moved her gaze from me to Ardella and back again. "You're famous."

"Famous?" I pointed to myself, eyes wide.

"She's exaggerating a little—but just a little." Ardella linked arms with me. "Come on. Let's get something to eat and we can talk about it."

"Eat?" I didn't eat.

Their faces fell.

"Oh. I forgot about that," Ardella said.

They glanced at each other.

"Well, I'm sure Gregor will provide for you," Marigold added. "Do you mind if we eat?"

"No, of course not."

They led me to a spot in the top of one of the tallest trees. It felt good to climb and be active in the fresh air. I never knew my assassin skills would come in handy, but I could remember scaling walls and walking across rooftops as I worked my way through the limbs and leaves. Maybe that was why I was so good at getting around without being noticed, I realized.

Marigold pulled a side-worn satchel over her head, where it had been hanging across her slim body. Inside was milk, honey, and small, round cakes.

We sat down, and the others shared the food while I looked around in amazement. I already felt stronger, even without feeding or resting. Being so close to nature restored me. I wondered what it would be like if I had stayed here, the way my father had wanted me to. Would it always be like this? Would I eventually stop needing to feed once I satisfied the fae side of me? I doubted it—being here for an hour or two was one thing, but, in the long term, I would need to feed. And that was where we would run into difficulty, I thought.

"So," Marigold said, licking honey from her fingertips. "What's it like to be a vampire?"

Ardella gasped sharply. "Mari."

"It's all right." I chuckled. "I don't mind talking about it. I would be interested, too."

"See?" Marigold gave her friend a triumphant smile and tossed back her blonde curls. "I didn't think she would mind."

I sat back against the trunk of the tree. "I'm not sure how to describe it. It's the only life I've ever known until recently."

"What's the city like?" Ardella asked. "Start there." She was just as eager to learn as Marigold was.

I smiled. "The city. I love the city, I have to admit. I miss it a little. It's so real. So vibrant. It's not always pretty, and it's nothing like this." I looked around, breathing deep of the fresh air. "The air is full of smog and smoke and the smells of cars and people and food. There's always a lot of noise, and everybody's in a hurry all the time."

"You don't make it sound very nice." Marigold frowned, reaching for another cake. "Why do you miss it if it's so messy?"

I shrugged. Not a bad question. "I guess because of the energy there. No, it's not always nice, but it's always interesting. And I do love the lights everywhere. They're beautiful, especially when you look at them from up high." My heart ached a little when I remembered gazing out over the city from Jonah's penthouse. I still felt a sharp, stinging bitterness toward him for dumping me like unwanted baggage.

"Do you have to feed all the time?" Marigold asked.

"Not all the time. When I feel weak or hungry, the way you do, I guess. But not as frequently."

"Do you sleep?"

"No."

"I would miss sleep," Ardella mused. "I love sleep." She looked serious, too, like she was thinking about the prospect of never sleeping again. And again, she resembled my sister. Whenever she was thinking seriously about something, even something hypothetical, she looked like her.

I giggled. "I envy you sometimes. I really do."

Marigold stood and stared out over the trees, her hands on her hips. "Sometimes I envy you."

"Why?"

"Because nothing exciting ever happens here. Not the way you described. There's never anything interested or exciting."

I laughed ruefully. "Excitement isn't all it's cracked up to be. I'm so tired of running around, never knowing what's going to happen next. I could use a little peace and quiet."

"Then it's a good thing you're here with us." Ardella smiled. She was radiant.

Marigold was beautiful, but Ardella shone. They were both gentle and sweet, and so kind.

At least Gregor had chosen nice companions for me.

ᔥ 3 0 ᔥ

ANISSA

I was resting in bed after two days in Avellane when Felicity came for me. I had been thinking about Sara, half-dreaming about being with her—as close to dreaming as a vampire could come. I'd allowed myself to sink into my thoughts and imagine I was with her. We were smiling and having fun, giggling over gossip about Jonah and Scott. Like two normal sisters would, chatting away about boys.

I'd been thinking about Jonah, of course, as well. And Allonic. And my mother. I longed for her more than I ever had when I thought she was dead. It was one thing to know I would never see her again, but another to be away from her when I knew she was out there somewhere. Just beyond my reach. Frustration didn't begin to describe the feeling.

I wanted all of them. I wanted to talk to them and be with them and have my family around me. More than anything, I wanted Jonah. I wasn't as angry with him anymore. I wanted to understand why he'd handed me over. I missed him so much, it hurt. When would we ever stop missing each other? When would we be together? I only wanted to be with him. It was that simple. Why did everything around us have to be complicated?

Felicity's entrance broke through the web of thoughts criss-crossing my mind. Rather than waiting for me to open the door or grant her entrance, she came in the room unannounced.

I sat up, feeling groggy. It was never easy to be torn from rest without warning. "What is it?" I asked, shaking my head to clear the fog.

"I'm sorry for disturbing you, but your father asked that I bring you to him."

"My father, huh?" I slid my feet into the leather-soled shoes provided for me and ran my hands through my hair, hoping I was in presentable condition. "It's about time."

"I try not to question his decisions," she said with a shrug. "Besides, he's been very busy. I'm sure he'll tell you more about it."

I could hardly wait.

We walked along the wood hall, artificial light streaming in through the carved-out windows. "What is the light made of? It's not sunlight, I know."

"That's a secret of ours," she said, just as tight-lipped as my father had been about it. I guessed I wasn't fae enough to share the secret, then. Would I ever fully fit in anywhere? The thought soured my mood a little.

Gregor was waiting for me when we entered his chambers. Why he couldn't have come for me himself, I didn't know. Maybe he was making a point that he couldn't be bothered to fetch me. Or he might have acted out of habit—he was powerful, after all, and not used to doing things for himself.

Once we were alone, he asked, "Are you comfortable here? Has everything been to your satisfaction?"

"Yes, right down to my guards." I enjoyed the discomfort on his face.

"They're not guards," he replied sourly.

"No, I do consider them friends now," I admitted, "but don't think I didn't see right through you sending them to me. I'm not dense."

"You have a habit of running away," he reminded me.

"I promise, I'm not this time." I wouldn't have done that in a million years, not when I had no idea what would happen to me once I left. The memory of fleeing from danger was too fresh. Sometimes, when I least expected it, I was back on the floor in that chamber at the Sanctuary. I wasn't in control of myself. The shades were hurting me. No, I wouldn't have run for anything.

"Come," he said. "I've been wanting to walk with you for days. Have your, erm... friends been showing you around?"

"A little," I said. "We've explored together."

"What do you think?"

"It's beautiful. I needed this. I feel rested and, well, complete in a way I'm not used to feeling."

"That's good to hear." He looked pleased and sounded that way, too. "I want you to feel as though you belong."

As we walked, he identified various landmarks. "That's where I meet with my advisors," he said, indicating a large, thick tree. "They live there. It's considered quite an honor."

"I'm sure it is."

He was showing off a little. I would allow it. I smiled indulgently as he pointed out their library, which contained all the documents pertaining to the settlement's history, and the cluster of trees in which they stored their food.

"Do you have seasons here?" I asked.

"Much milder than the ones in the human world," he explained. "Our winter is short and not nearly as cold, but it does affect the amount of honey the bees can make. They sleep when they get too cold, you know, and honey is one of our main staples. We have a system in place to keep them warm throughout the year."

It was fascinating to learn more about the little world they'd created for themselves, a self-sustaining environment in which they needed nothing and no one else. It was safer that way. And they were happy—everywhere I went, I saw smiles. I heard laughter, like the tinkling of tiny bells, floating on the breeze that ruffled my hair and skimmed over the fabric of my robes.

"You know, I can't think about winter without thinking about your mother." He sighed, stopping in the middle of a bridge. He leaned on one of the thick vines used as a railing, looking out over the hundreds of trees around us. He took a deep breath, letting it out slowly. "She loved winter. We would walk in the snow for hours—neither of us felt the weather as keenly as humans, so it didn't matter if the wind blew or the snow was blinding. We walked, arm in arm. Sometimes, it felt like we were alone in the world, only the two of us, when everyone else was inside. And the snow made the sounds of our footsteps disappear. Everything softened. It almost seemed wrong to say a word and break the silence.

There was so much love left in him for her. And she was alive. And I knew it. But I couldn't tell him. I looked away, hoping to hide the guilt in my eyes. He didn't notice. He was lost in his memories.

"I've never been one for snow, but I was willing to put up with it if it made her happy. I've always preferred spring and summer—as you can see." He smiled a little, glancing at me from the corner of his eye. "It was another thing we felt differently about, but it didn't matter. There was enough love between us that we could get through little things like that. And everything seemed like a little thing, if that makes any sense."

I thought about Jonah. Yes, it made perfect sense. I had fallen in love with him even when I knew it was wrong, that he was from an enemy clan. Even though I was supposed to kill him. Against all odds, we had found each other. Nothing else mattered very much in the face of the way we felt.

"You miss her," I mused.

"Of course, I do. Every day. I suppose it's the same for you."

I nodded, unable to speak over the lump in my throat. He deserved to know, but I wasn't the one to tell him. I hoped he could forgive me if he ever found out I knew and kept it to myself. What would he think if he found out she had turned into something between a vampire and a shade? Would he still love her? Maybe it was better to leave him with his memories, in which my mother was beautiful and perfect. Nothing could touch those remembrances, I was sure.

I wouldn't ruin those for him.

31

ANISSA

The next day, I knew what I had to do. I'd rested and hidden out, but hiding wasn't my style. So, after meeting up with Ardella and Marigold, I went to his chambers without being summoned and knocked on the door.

"Come in."

I stepped inside to find him studying old scrolls. I wondered about the long hours he kept. What was he working on? Whatever it was, it seemed very important. Hadn't Felicity told me so? He was busy with something. He wouldn't tell me what it was. Just another thing he felt he'd best keep from me.

He smiled when he looked up to find me there. "This is a pleasant surprise."

"I don't think you'll find it so pleasant when I tell you what I've come for," I admitted with a sad smile.

"You're wearing the clothes you arrived in," he observed.

I ran my hands over the top and pants, freshly cleaned. I couldn't imagine how long it had taken to get the dirt and blood out of them, but they looked as good as new. "Yes, I am."

He put away his scroll with a sad, heavy sigh. "I know what that means. I suppose I should be glad you didn't run away this time."

"I didn't want to lie to you or run from you. I don't want to give you the impression I'm anything less than grateful for what you've done for me." I'd practiced my speech throughout the night, shortening it until I was certain he couldn't interrupt me before I'd gotten my message across.

I expected him to fight me on it. I expected him to tell me I was crazy if I thought he was going to let me go, when I had argued over and over that Jonah and I were in such trouble. I was sure he would use my words against me.

Instead, he merely nodded. "I understand."

That was a surprise. "You do?"

He nodded, sitting on a log stool as he did. "I know what it's like to want to follow your heart, even when others tell you that you shouldn't. I know what it's like to have everything and everyone against you, when you feel like there are insurmountable obstacles in your path." His eyes met mine, and I saw sadness sparkling in them. "I don't want to be one of those obstacles."

My heart opened to him. I knelt at his feet, taking his hands in mind. "I don't want you to ever feel like you're one, either. I owe you so much."

"I should have given you more. I should have had the strength you have. You're so like your mother—maybe a little too much like her."

My heart ached again when he mentioned her.

He continued, "She rushed into things without worrying about what others thought. She didn't have a father bearing down on her, either, or the certainty she was neglecting her duty by being with me. Still, if she had, I think she would've wanted to be with me anyway. She had courage. I didn't."

"It takes courage to give up what you want," I reminded him. "Not everybody can turn their back on what they want in favor of their duty."

He smiled and ran a hand over the side of my face. "You're so like her. You have her heart, too. I wonder if you got anything from me at all." He touched my hair. "Besides this."

I giggled. "I'm sure there's plenty of you inside me."

"That reminds me." He stood up and rang a bell.

I rose to my feet as Felicity entered

"Bring me one of the casters," he said.

She didn't ask questions but instead hurried away.

"A spell caster?" I asked, more than a little apprehensive.

He nodded firmly. "I can't send you out into the world again unprotected."

"What will the caster do?"

"Protect you, of course. You'll receive the same sort of enchantment placed on you when you were born. It's to hide your fae blood, so you're not as easily trackable."

My heart swelled, and I threw my arms around him without thinking about it. After a moment's pause, I felt his arms wrap around me.

He held me, stroking the top of my head, and I made a promise to myself that I would come back to him.

Felicity cleared her throat, and I stepped away from my father.

The spell caster entered—I hadn't been sure what to expect and was glad to see another fae like any of the rest. A little older, maybe, but the same otherwise. I closed my eyes as he cast the spell, speaking ancient words I didn't understand. I waited to feel different, but when the spell was finished, I seemed unchanged. That made sense—I hadn't felt any different when the old spell wore off, had I?

"How do I know when the enchantment starts to fade?" I asked when I opened my eyes. "I didn't know last time."

Gregor's rueful smile told me what I needed to know before he said a word. "You'll know when they start hunting you again."

32

PHILIPPA

I'd gathered the vampires of our clan downstairs in the basement.

"Thank you for meeting here with me again on such short notice." I looked around the assembly room at the hundreds of faces staring back at me, intent, waiting for instructions. "I know things have been up in the air lately, and I hope we can manage to settle them soon."

Scott was there, standing up front. It was good to see him, good to know he supported me. Once he had come back with Sara—they had gone searching for Gage, after all—we'd discussed what I should say next. I had to be diplomatic, careful with the words I used. I didn't want to start a war or even a skirmish.

"I wanted you all to know Gage has been found."

I braced myself for the flow of questions, exclamations, demands to know more. It was natural. They wanted to know where he was. Of course, they did. I waited for it to die down before I said another word.

"He's all right," I told them, holding my hands up to get them to quiet down. "I've seen him myself, and we talked, and he's well. We can call off the search. Thank you all for the work you put into seeking him."

"What about Jonah?" one of them called out, and a chorus of voices joined in.

My heart sank.

"I'm sure he's fine, too. There's nothing to worry about." I only wished I believed that. I understood it was important to tell them what they needed to hear, although if it wasn't necessarily true.

Jonah. Where are you? I need you right now. I need my big brother, my best friend. I need you with me. Why did you walk away? Aren't we important to you anymore?

I couldn't help but glance at Scott again, and his smile bolstered me a little. I could rely on him, at least for the time being—when he wasn't wrapped up in Sara. My eyes fell on her, too, since she was right beside him. Where else would she be? I couldn't help noticing there was something different about her, but I couldn't put my finger on what exactly. She appeared the same—same face, same hair, that sort of thing. Maybe it was the expression on her face, or the way she carried herself. Her head was a little higher than usual, her shoulders back a little farther. She was more confident. Maybe that was it. I couldn't quite figure it out.

I shifted my focus out over the crowd. "Thanks again. If anything else further develops, I'll let you know." They didn't seem satisfied, and I couldn't shake the feeling I was letting them down, but there was nothing else for me to do. I watched as they walked away and hoped I hadn't done something wrong.

Scott helped me down from the table, and I considered asking him if Sara was okay but then thought twice about it. He might accuse me of being catty, when that was the last thing I was trying to be. I only wanted to be sure she was all right—if she was spending time with my brother, I needed to know she was okay.

"You did a good job," he said.

"I wish I felt like I did." I looked around at the dispersing crowd and remembered the last time I'd spoken to them like this, when I sent them out to look for my brother. Then, I'd felt a strong energy coming from them. We had been together, united in a task. I'd felt strong and capable. All I felt now was like a failure.

Vance had been here that first time. I couldn't help scanning the room for him, searching for his hoodie. I almost wished he had sneaked in to watch me again. But no. I didn't see him as the room emptied out. My heart sank even further. I wasn't sure it could get any lower than it was.

"We're going back up to the penthouse. You coming?" Scott took Sara's hand. I couldn't help feeling a little jealous. They had each other. All I had was Vance, who I'd left at the cathedral and over-possessive Sledge. Vance might have been torn to ribbons by that female vampire's claws for all I knew. She seemed like the type.

I shook my head. "I don't think so. I need to walk. There's too much up here right now." I pointed to my head.

"Are you sure you'll be safe?"

"Plenty sure. I'll see you later." I walked out, desperate for fresh air—as fresh as it could get in Manhattan, anyway. I went straight to the hall just off the assembly room, running my hand along the wall as I did. I was alone. Nobody saw when I found the single brick that was out of place. I pressed that brick, and a doorway opened up, a segment of the wall sliding back to reveal the alley beside the building. With one more look around me, I slipped out, closing the wall behind.

"Took you long enough."

I jumped in surprise, whirling around with my hand over my chest, my teeth bared.

Vance smiled down at me, and I wished my heart wouldn't skip a beat every time he appeared like this.

"Thanks for scaring me half to death," I breathed, bending a little at the waist with my hands on my knees. "Was that your plan?"

"Something like that." There was no humor in his voice.

"Well, thanks. And thanks for potentially stirring up trouble by being here." I straightened up, placing my hands on his chest with the intention of pushing him away.

Instead, he caught my wrists and held them tight. We stared each other down for what felt like forever, with me wishing all the while the butterflies in my stomach would calm down.

He released me, taking a step back. I looked him up and down.

"Where's your girl?" I asked.

"Where's your guy?"

I winced. "Why are you here?"

His expression changed. He wasn't trying to antagonize me anymore. That one little shift was enough to strike fear in my heart.

"He's gone."

"What?" My pulse froze. "You mean Gage?"

He nodded. "I thought you'd want to know."

"I don't get it." And I had told everyone inside he was safe. Damn it. I leaned against the wall, one hand on my forehead. It was all too much. "Where would he go? Do you know? Did he tell you?"

"Remember, I wasn't supposed to know he was there. He would never tell me where he was going."

I stood up straight and tall, hands on my hips. "Oh, really? You don't know what your father did to him?"

He blinked. "What makes you think he did anything? What's this all about?"

I tried to decide if he meant it, or if he was playing dumb. He was pretty good at that. But no, I knew him well enough to know when he meant it. And he meant it. He had no idea what I was talking about. He still thought his father was honorable. I had the feeling his bubble would burst someday soon.

"I can't believe this. He wouldn't run. Not after..." I stopped speaking when I realized how close I was to revealing his plan.

"It's just impossible," I muttered. How would I find him? Who was he with? It was sheer luck that brought me to him in the first place.

Vance shrugged. "I'm only telling you what I know. Like I said, I thought you would want to know, too." He turned like he was ready to leave.

I couldn't let him go like this, so I reached out and touched his arm.

"Why are you moving to New York? I mean, really. Why are you doing it?" I wanted him to tell me he was breaking free of his father. After what Gage told me, I hated to think of Vance being part of his clan's business even by name.

"Will you keep it a secret?"

The breath caught in my throat. Not what I had expected to hear. "Sure."

He looked around like he was making sure we were alone before replying. When he did, he leaned closer. I was up against the wall. I could go no farther. He placed one hand just above my head and loomed over me. I hated the way my knees went weak.

"I'm taking a position with the League's Special Ops Unit."

I was speechless. Law enforcement? Special Ops? Him? Talk about the last vampire I would ever consider a candidate for a position like that. When I regained the ability to speak, I sputtered, "Why's it a secret?"

He pressed his lips together, sighing through his nose. "Because I'll be undercover."

"Undercover?" That added a whole other level to the job. I was a little worried for him—it sounded rather dangerous. "Does your father know?"

He shook his head. "He would try to block it if he did. I know him."

"How can he not know? He's head of the league, right?"

"Right, but only the identity of the head of the Special Ops Unit is known to the league. It's an old rule they put in place ages ago. It keeps the members of the unit from potential corruption or collusion."

Well, that made me a lot more confident in the leadership we had in place. Was there even a potential for such a thing? Would they stoop to collusion or worse, if necessary?

He continued, "Meanwhile, on the inside, we only know the other guys on our team and the one member we answer to directly. Our handler. Otherwise, the way the organizational ladder is set up isn't something we're privy to. They keep us in the dark for a reason."

"Wow," I breathed. It was the only thing that seemed to sum up how I felt. Undercover. Secrecy. It was enough to take my breath away.

"Now you know. And like I said, I expect you to keep it a secret."

I nodded, chewing my lip. "There's one more question I need you to answer." When he nodded, I asked, "Will you be in danger?"

A smile played over his lips. "And if I said yes, would that persuade you to see me again? You know, just in case something was to happen?"

I had to laugh. "You're the worst, you know? You can never drop it, can you?"

"No, ma'am."

I looked him in the eye, prepared to tell him off once and for all. That little performance in the tower had only reminded me of why I'd dumped him. But instead of exploding on him like I wanted, a single tear overflowed onto my cheek.

"We already tried once, remember?" I asked in a shaky voice. I felt my chin trembling as I struggled to maintain composure. "I won't be a fool twice. Do you understand what I'm trying to say? For once and for all. I won't let you hurt me again."

He gave me a sad smile as he touched the tear that had landed on my cheek.

I gasped a little in the back of my throat at the surge of electricity that passed between his fingertips and my face.

I wanted his touch more than anything—except never letting him hurt me again.

He didn't say a word, not even to defend himself. He only slid his finger over my skin as he trailed the tear down to my jaw.

EPILOGUE

VANCE

I took off, leaving her behind, and, with her, I left the key to my heart, to my soul.

This redheaded beauty I gave my heart to ages ago kills me. She downright kills me.

I never cheated on Philippa. Hell, I couldn't have. Not a chance.

But I had to get her out of my life at that point. I had to do what I needed in order to keep her safe from anyone who meant her harm.

So, I let her think I cheated. I've always let her think that.

Things have changed.

Now, I can be with her and I know I can keep her safe.

Except there seems to be another in the competition for her heart—Sledge.

I punched a brick wall, wishing it was the burly vampire who clearly was head over heels for my girl.

She'd always be my girl.

Hopefully, one day, she'll see it.

Keep reading for an excerpt from the next book in the *League of Vampires*.

RYE BREWER

ABSOLUTION

LEAGUE OF VAMPIRES

ABSOLUTION

Ancient enemies, newfound coalitions.
Anissa's not about to take Jonah's decision to face his enemies alone. This former slayer isn't your average sit on the sidelines kind of girl.

⚜

New heroes, not so new archenemies.
Fane wants forgiveness and allegiance, but not at the cost of the ones he loves most. Certainly, not at the expense of an new soul that is joining his cadre.

⚜

Needs rarely line up with wants.
Philippa's feelings for Vance won't be the end of her, but will they be the end of a loved one

CHAPTER 1

JONAH

Images flashed through my mind, based on what Fane had told me.

His words rang in my ears still. *"It goes back centuries, the history I have with Lucian. All the way back to when I was a human, named Dommik."*

Dommik. When he'd been my father. Not Fane, the vampire legend that he was now

His words and those images in my mind mixed with memories of my childhood, back when I was human. We had been so happy. We were still happy after we'd been turned—and I could remember that clearly, like the end of one life and the beginning of another—but it was a different sort of happiness.

We couldn't live simply anymore. We had a clan to think about. A much bigger family than what we'd known before then.

And all because of Lucian's hatred and obsession.

The cool air suddenly felt freezing cold. Even the brand on my arm barely registered on my consciousness, which was saying something, seeing as how the burning was all I could think about when it first appeared and flared up, as if a design had been burned into my skin with a cattle branding iron.

There had been times when Lucian seemed fake, hadn't there?

When his smile had faltered a little, or I'd seen emptiness in his eyes. That last meeting of the League of Vampires, the way he'd stood there like a deity, absorbing the appreciation of the vampires in attendance. False modesty.

I tried to tell myself I was only remembering things through the lens of what Fane —who I'd recently learned was my father— had told me. It was easy to do that, wasn't it? To let new information color memories? I had to be fair. Didn't I?

Yet... Lucian had turned my mother into a vampire. He set my family on its path, changed the direction of our lives.

Sure, I would be long dead by now if he hadn't, but I would've lived a human life. As complicated as humans thought their lives were, their issues were nothing compared to what we vampires faced. There had been times, especially after losing my parents, when I'd wished we'd never been turned. I wouldn't have had to live endless decades never knowing what happened to the people I loved most in the world.

Fane didn't try to comfort me or ask if I had any questions. He only stared at me the way a father would gaze at his son after missing so much of his life.

"I'm staring," he said with a slight smile. "I'm sorry."

"It's all right. It doesn't bother me." I studied him.

Funny how he resembled my father and sounded like my father but was different. Something about his eyes, maybe, or the way he held himself. A hardness? What had he seen since he left us?

"Where is the h—the girl?"

He'd almost called Anissa the half-breed again—I could tell—but stopped himself in time.

I decided to let it pass.

"With her father. She's safe there."

"You're sure about that?"

"Of course. I wouldn't want her to be anywhere I wasn't sure of her safety. I sent her there to be certain she's not part of whatever happens next."

The lines on his brow deepened when he frowned. "You do care for her, don't you?"

"You doubted it?" Anissa was part-vampire, part-fae and the most amazing woman I'd ever met.

"I didn't know if it was infatuation or real attachment."

"I'm not a baby anymore," I reminded him with a faint smile. "I've grown up a lot."

He nodded. "It's easy to forget that after all this time apart."

All this time.

Decades.

Even so, the memory of the pain remained fresh. I would never forget the way life had stopped during those first days, when my siblings and I realized our parents had vanished. No explanation, no clue where they'd gone. Nothing mattered, when all we could think about was our parents and what might've happened to them. We'd lived in a sort of limbo where the world kept turning, but we stayed still. And none of us had ever been the same after. Especially not Philippa.

Which brought me to the next matter at hand. "You have to see her."

His eyebrows shot up. "What? Who?"

I stood and stared at him. "Philippa. You have to see her."

He appeared defeated. "No. I don't."

"Then at least let me tell her you're still alive."

He shook his head. "Jonah, I already told you how dangerous that is. Remember? The fewer of you who know I'm alive, the better. I only stayed away this long because I wanted to protect you—I can't turn my back on the promise I made to myself. If all these years of hiding away were wasted and something were to happen to any of you anyway, I would never forgive myself."

I glared at him. "I understand. I do. I spent years as head of the clan. I know there are almost no decisions that are easy. There's always a drawback or a compromise."

"Not an easy lesson to learn."

"It isn't," I agreed. "I learned it the hard way, over and over."

He nodded with an understanding smile. "So you see, then. Being away from you all has been torture. It didn't get any easier as time went on."

There was pain written all over his face.

I tried to imagine having kids and forcing myself to be away from them. Not merely being apart, but with full knowledge they thought I was dead. It would crush me.

Then again, it had crushed *us*, never knowing for sure. Especially my sister.

"It didn't get any easier for us, either, you know. Especially Philippa." I stared hard at him to get my point across. "She changed. She'll never go back to being the girl she used to be."

A shadow crossed his face. "What do you mean?"

"You remember how she used to be—bright, fun, funny. Always teasing and joking. High-spirited."

"She was a joy," he murmured.

I knew he was thinking back on the way she could always make him laugh, no matter what sort of mood he was in. They used to go on and on for hours, playing word games, debating, challenging each other.

She was so quick, so wily. But those qualities were on the surface. She was a brilliant judge of character, too, even at a young age. It was what made her the ideal advisor for me—she would've been his advisor, if he had stayed.

"All that brightness and sweetness went away when you did. I'm not trying to heap guilt on you. I'm really not. But you need to know. She found a way to move on. We all did. We didn't have a choice. And it changed us all, but none of us changed as much as she did. She has an edge. She's jaded. She doesn't trust the way she used to." My eyes narrowed. "You owe her this much. She deserves to know you're alive."

He stared off into the distance. "You said it yourself—sometimes there are difficult decisions to be made. Maybe this will give her some measure of peace, but at what cost? Her safety? Her life?" He raised his hand, as if saying *halt*. "I can't allow that."

I shook my head. "I can't go back and face her—ever—with this lie hanging over me. I can't betray her that way. She still loves you so much. You were her hero."

"The me I used to be," he uttered. "That's not who I am anymore."

"Why don't you let her be the one to decide that? She'll be so glad you're alive it won't matter."

It seemed like he was almost ready to give in—I knew the look. He was fighting with himself.

I used the opportunity to gain the upper hand, perhaps twisting the knife a little. "I'll help find Gage if you go see her."

"What?" His eyes dilated—the sole sign of his surprise.

"I'll help, but only if you agree to see Philippa."

He folded his arms. "Blackmail?"

"If it works, yes."

He turned away.

I was getting more desperate. "What can I say to get you to understand how important this is? Please. All I can do is ask you to please do this. It'll mean so much."

"What if...?" His voice broke, and he cleared his throat. "What if she doesn't want to see me? What if she hates me for what I did? She always had a temper, and she wasn't good at letting go of a grudge."

I pressed my lips together to keep from smiling. "That's something that hasn't changed."

"Sometimes, I think it would be easier to remember her before, the way things were, when she didn't hate me."

"I never said she hated you. She doesn't hate you."

"You don't know that. It would be better for her to look back at me the way I was before. She will probably hate me when she finds out. I'm not sure you don't."

I ignored that. I wasn't going to tell him I hated him. I wasn't going to tell him I didn't.

Though I didn't.

With every passing day, I was learning we often had to make decisions that weren't always easy.

That hit home for me now, stronger than ever, knowing I'd sent Anissa to Avellane to be with Gregor, her father and leader of the fae, knowing she would be pissed. Hopefully, she didn't hate me—wouldn't hate me. But still...

He watched me, waiting for a reply, wanting to know.

I gave him one. "Anything is better than not knowing."

His gaze was steady. "Where should we meet?"

"It's been a long time since I've stood here." Fane walked to the edge of the roof after stepping through the portal behind me and gazed out over the city.

It was a night like any other—down there, at least.

Not where I stood.

He took a deep breath. "I've missed being here. That's for sure." He glanced at me from the corner of his eye and smiled. "I spent a lot of time looking over the city, thinking about things whenever I needed to clear my head. I didn't dare come back."

"I understand that."

"I hope your sister does, too." He seemed nervous for the first time since we met again.

He wasn't Fane at that moment. It was like being with my father again.

I looked around. Just because we were on the roof didn't mean we were safe from prying eyes. "You'd better stay out of sight up here. I don't want anyone seeing you—as either Dommik Bourke, previous leader of the Bourke clan, or Fane."

"Wouldn't it be better for me to wait inside, then?"

I shook my head. "I'll go talk to her first—to warm her up. Please, stay here. Don't leave."

"I'll be right here when you're ready."

I hoped he meant it. I would hate to go through what I knew

Philippa was going to put me through for him to not be here when I came back for him.

There was noise inside the penthouse. It wasn't as empty as it was when I was last here.

I listened closely.

Philippa's chambers.

I hoped she was alone.

It occurred to me as I crossed the living area and walked down the hall that I hadn't seen her since leaving the league meeting.

I braced myself for what was to come.

She didn't notice me at first. Her back was to the open door. There was a backpack on the bed, open, and she was shoving things into it, right and left.

I caught a peek when she moved to the side.

Weapons. Several daggers, two handguns, two throwing stars.

She bundled dark clothes in there, too. Jeans, a sweatshirt, a sweater, tees—all in dark gray or black.

I hadn't known my fashion-conscious sister owned that much plain, dark clothing.

I cleared my throat, and she spun around.

Her posture was defensive, like she was ready for a fight.

I held my hands up. "It's just me."

Her fists dropped to her sides. "Oh, Jonah!" she breathed, and, in the blink of an eye, she was throwing herself at me and squeezing me around the neck until I could hardly breathe.

"Easy, easy," I groaned.

"Where have you been? I didn't think I'd ever see you again!" She pulled away, holding me at arm's length so she could take me in. "What have you been doing? Where did you go?"

"One thing at a time. What are you doing? What are you packing for?" I glanced at the backpack. "I mean, it looks a little... stockpiled?"

"I'm so glad you're back. I have a million things to tell you." She hurried back to the bed and finished wedging clothes into it before closing the zipper.

"You picked the perfect time to return. I have an errand, so you can take back being the leader and keep these hooligans in line."

"Wait a minute. I'm not here to lead the clan."

She stopped and turned slowly toward me. "What's that again?" Her hands were planted on her hips, and her chin jutted out.

"I'm sorry, but that's not why I came back here. Besides, I don't think it's as easy as just walking back in and saying something like, 'Hey, I'm back.'"

She still appeared annoyed, but one corner of her mouth disappeared as she chewed on it. "I guess you're right. Well, I'm still glad you're here. I'm glad I get to see you and know you're alive."

Her words hit me like a ton of bricks. It hadn't been fair for me to run off without a word—the way our parents had.

"I'm sorry I put you through that. Really. Have you ever, I don't know, just got caught up in the moment? Did you ever do something you wouldn't think you were capable of otherwise?"

She sighed. "Yes. I can't lie." She glanced at her backpack.

I looked at it, too. "What kind of errand are you going on that you need all that? I saw the weapons, so don't pretend you didn't pack them."

She shook her head the tiniest bit, as if fortifying herself for the answer. "You're just going to try to talk me out of it."

"Depends on what it is."

"No, I know you. You'll try to tell me it's wrong."

"Which makes me wonder even more." I frowned. "Tell me."

"What if I told you it has to do with Gage? Like... finding him?" She slid the backpack onto one shoulder then leaned into it as she guided the second strap on.

"Hold on, hold on." I blocked the doorway. "Seriously? You think you're going to go searching for him?"

She blinked then regained her composure. "You think you're going to stop me?"

"No. I know better, and I don't have the time to waste, either. I need you to stop and think about this first, is all. This is a big job, you know? It's dangerous."

"I know. Since when do I ever back down from danger?"

"Never. That's what's worrying me the most."

She tossed her red hair.

I watched it cascade over her backpack. How many times had I seen her do that when she was determined to do something?

Her eyes were piercing, the set of her jaw firm. "You're not the only one who's been wrapped up in doing things lately, you know. I've really surprised myself in the last few days."

I smiled. "I believe it. You always rise to the challenge."

"I have to go now," she whispered. "I'm sorry if you don't like the idea."

"There's something I need you to do first. It might even make things a little easier for you."

She raised a brow. "What do you mean?"

I took her by the hand and led her out into the main room, still dark and otherwise empty, toward the glass doors.

"Come on. Trust me."

"Is it Gage?"

"No."

She made a sound, something like a sigh of frustration—or anger. "Anissa? Is Anissa out there? Is she with you? Because I don't think visiting with her is worth spending time on right now."

When would she ever come around on Anissa? "Stop asking so many questions and come. Anissa is safe where she is."

"Wait." She stopped, still shy of the doors. "You left her somewhere? That doesn't sound like you. I thought you two were attached at the hip."

I rolled my eyes at the sarcasm in her voice. "Yeah, well, there are things going on right now she doesn't need to be part of. I don't want her getting hurt or... anything."

I pulled her again, and the muscles in my forearm flexed—

which made my brand sting more than ever. I didn't bother saying anything about it to her.

I was already about to drop a bomb on Philippa, she didn't need to be concerned with the brand as well.

"Come on."

I walked her outside and hoped Fane was still out there.

The wind blew my and Philippa raised a hand to brush a thick, red strand from in front of her face as a dark figure emerged from the shadows.

I stepped back.

She froze, eyes trained on him as he came closer.

"I don't believe it." Her voice was barely a whisper.

"Philippa." His jaw clenched.

She shook her head. "No. This is impossible."

CHAPTER 2

JONAH

I waited to see what she would do. It was like waiting for an animal to make a move—would there be an attack? Would it back down?

She threw herself at him, arms closing around his neck. "Is it really you?"

"It's me." He hugged her gently, like he was afraid she would break.

All sorts of conflicting emotions raced across his face before he pulled out of their embrace and stepped back. Their embrace had lasted the time it had taken me to blink. Not nearly long enough.

I groaned quietly to myself.

Then he turned to me. "All right. She knows. Can we go now?"

She stared. "Wait. What's wrong? You just got here."

"Yes, but we have something important to do now."

I winced. Didn't he have a clue how he sounded?

Her face worked as she processed this. "Are you serious? You're going to do this to me right now?"

I stepped forward, wishing he'd been a little gentler with her. Maybe bringing him home hadn't been a good idea, after all. It was one thing to think her father was dead, but another for him to reject her with no explanation.

I put a hand on her arm, wanting to comfort her—or maybe keep her from doing anything rash. "I wanted you to see him. I didn't want to keep it from you that he was alive."

She glared at me like I was the one who had broken her heart. "You choose now to tell me? You're going to do this to me when there's so much going on? You bring him here like it's no big deal?" Then, she whirled on Fane. "And you! You just show up out of nowhere, after all this time? And you don't think to come to us and tell us you're alive? Jonah had to *bring* you here?"

Only she wasn't angry with him. She was hurt and confused. I could hear it in her voice and remembered feeling the same way myself at first.

He sighed. "Philippa, I can explain."

She held up a hand, and her head hung low. "Please. This is too much at once. I can't understand why this is happening right now. I mean, all this time? All this time!" Her head snapped up again, and she glared at him. "How could you not tell us you were alive? How could you let us think you were dead?"

"Please. I want to tell you everything, but you have to give me a chance—and we don't have much time."

"I don't have much time, either. Holy hell!" She threw her hands up and spun around then paced back and forth, shaking her head and cursing the entire time. "This is ridiculous. You walk back into our lives like it's nothing, you show up after all this time and I'm supposed to, what? Hug you? Cry? Tell you how happy I am you're alive even though I've spent all these years trying to get used to the idea of you being dead? Is that what you want from me? Is it?"

"I don't want anything from you," he said. "Anything at all. It means so much to see you like this... You look well."

"Yeah, so do you." She peered at me then back at him. "So? Are you back, as in back forever? Have you decided to be part of the clan again?"

"No, that can never be. I don't live in this world anymore." He glanced at me for help.

"Philippa... this is Fane." I held my breath and waited.

Her face contorted in disbelief as she shook her head so hard her hair flipped back and forth over her shoulders. "No. That can't be true. Not our father. Fane isn't a normal creature. I mean, he's practically a myth. This?" She gestured to him. "This is Dommik Bourke."

"It's true, Philippa." His voice was firm, sharp.

Her head snapped around to face him.

"This is who I am."

"How? How could you do that? How?" she shrieked. "You're somebody else now? You simply stepped out of your life and decided to be someone else? Like we didn't matter? And now you're, what? Some secretive nomad vigilante or whoever Fane is supposed to be? While we—" She clasped her hands in front of her chest when her voice cracked, then broke. "While we thought you were gone?"

He closed his eyes. "I can't make up for this, but it wasn't my choice. We had no choice."

"Mother?" she whispered through tears.

He shook his head.

Her body quaked with sobs she kept silent. After a few deep breaths, she spoke again. "Gage is missing. Things are crazy right now."

Fane nodded. "I know."

"You know? How could you?"

He smiled for the first time—a faint smile, but it was there. "I've been watching over things from a distance."

"Right. Because that's what *Fane* does," she muttered.

She was starting to slide off into anger again, which nothing but a waste of time.

I intervened. "Okay. There's a lot we have to do, and we can't spend all our time with accusations."

"I agree," Fane said, his eyes still on her. "Tell me what you know about Gage. What have you've learned?"

"I found out why he ran away," she replied with her head high. "I have a reliable source who told me where I could find him. He was hiding at the league headquarters for a while."

Fane's expression hardened at the mention of the headquarters—as did mine, since I'd learned of Lucian's role in our family's history.

She went on, oblivious. "I went there and talked with him in the woods."

"Did anybody overhear you?"

"No, he insisted we go very far away. He said... He said he had a job to do. There were a lot of wild accusations." She shook her head. "I'm still not sure if he was in his right mind, honestly. Only now, he's gone again, and Vance has vanished, too."

"What has Vance got to do with it?" Fane asked.

I was on guard, too, seeing as how Vance was Lucian's son.

She lowered her gaze. "He was helping me for a little while, but my source tells me he's gone."

"And who is this source?"

"I can't tell you." She lifted her gaze to him. "I'm sorry. I owe them a lot and don't want to get them tangled up."

"Fine, then. I have my own contacts and can reach out to them." He faced me. "I want you with me on this."

"Wait! You're going to look for him?" Just like that, she turned into the little sister who felt left out when our father wanted to include her big brothers—but not her—in a mission. "What about me? That's what I was going to do."

"You stay here." He went to her, taking her arms in his hands. "I want you as far from this as can be. You have to stay safe—not only for yourself, but for the clan. Keep things together here."

Her shoulders slumped. "All right, I guess." Her eyes went to the backpack by her feet.

I felt sorry for her. She was all ready to go, and we showed up and changed her plans.

There were voices nearby, loud enough to hear. The three of us ducked into the shadows.

"Scott," I murmured. "Should we tell him?"

"That I'm alive?" Fane asked.

"No. Don't do it," Philippa whispered vehemently.

Both of us stared at her in surprise.

"How can you say that?" I asked. "How would you feel if you knew I was keeping him from you?"

"It's not about that," she said. "It's about Sara."

"What about her?"

"I don't trust her."

"Oh, come on." I rolled my eyes. "This again? What do you have against her? You really have to get over this."

"It's not personal, even though I don't like her," she said hotly. "I feel she's hiding something. And if that's true, she shouldn't know about Fane."

Fane nodded. "That's the sort of decision a leader makes. We have to think about all the possibilities."

My sister practically glowed at the compliment.

"Did you tell her?" she asked.

There was only one *her* she could mean—Anissa.

"No, I didn't. Well, I told her I met Fane, but I didn't say anything about him being my father."

"Right now, Gage is our top priority," Fane said. "He's in danger. Scott can wait." He glanced at me. "And then we can sort out the other things, too. After Gage is taken care of."

"What other things?" Philippa appeared hurt. "What else haven't you told me?" Her eyes darted back and forth between us.

He beheld me.

I stared back.

Neither of us said anything. I knew he wanted to protect her, and so did I.

"Great. Just great." She stepped back, away from us. "Go off and run around the whole world together. See if I care. I'll be here, holding down the fort, making sure you have a clan to come back to. I'm not special enough for you to clue in. No problem." She picked up her backpack and stormed off, back inside the penthouse.

I lunged forward, wanting to stop her, but Fane grabbed me and held me firmly.

"She'll get over it. It's for the best," he said. "I don't want her involved in what we're going to do."

"What are we going to do... now that you mention it?"

"You said you'd help me find Gage. First things first. We have to go now. We've spent too much time here already." He cast a portal. "Come on."

I turned to where Philippa had gone inside. I wished I had time to tell her I was sorry about excluding her.

We needed to be on our game, all of us, if we were going to get through what was coming.

She couldn't sulk or, worse, take things in her own hands to show us how valuable she was.

Fane might have forgotten how she could be at times, but I hadn't.

"Jonah. We need to go, now. Your brother needs us."

Right.

My brother.

The one in actual danger.

That pressed me into a decision, and I stepped through the portal.

CHAPTER 3

ANISSA

I t was weird, being back in the human world after running around between realms for so long.

Nothing was the same as it used to be while I walked in the city—once my city, not long ago, but yet forever ago—head down, hood up, fists jammed into the pockets of my sweatshirt.

It was as though overnight, I'd gone back to the person—the assassin—I used to be, dodging crowds of people on the street, doing my best to blend in, even as I walked with purpose.

People had no idea.

That was the funny part.

Those humans with their TV shows and lattes and little dramas. They didn't know how much went on right under their noses or over their heads. They were oblivious to what really made the world spin—and how close they'd come to extinction if the forces all around them decided to go to war.

Better to let them go on thinking they were the masters of their universe.

A light rain fell, creating a mist around me as I dashed up the wide stone stairs of one of the city's oldest and most ornate libraries. If I was going to find my best friend, Raze, it would be at the library. He never could get enough of learning about humans, and he knew better than to keep too many of their books in his rooms at the mansion.

Marcus, leader of the Carver clan, and his deep core of suspicion wouldn't allow for that. I had visited the library with Raze before and seen the way the college girls stared at him over the tops and sides of their books when they knew he wasn't looking. They'd whisper to each other about him while he sat there with his head buried, lost in another world.

Though I'd never wanted him that way, I used to sneer nastily to myself, knowing how fast they'd change their minds if they knew what he really was.

The inside of the building was a giant maze full of the smell of paper and people. I glanced around, wondering where he could be. He usually tried to find a quiet nook to hide out in, away from eyes and whispering voices.

I scanned the area, up and down the rows and stacks. It took me a few minutes, but eventually I spotted him, sitting alone in a leather chair, a thick book in his lap. His head was down, his eyes riveted to the page.

I couldn't help but smile a little. How many times had I seen him sitting exactly like that? The library could come down around his head and he wouldn't blink.

My assassin's mind woke up from its sleep—it had been weeks since my last mission—and reminded me that anybody could come up and take him out if they wanted to. He wouldn't fight back. Would he? The thought set my heart racing, although I reminded myself it was only a thought. Nobody would hurt Raze. There was no reason to.

Still, his absorption made it easy for me to sneak up behind him.

He didn't even flinch when I leaned in and whispered in his ear. "Read any good books lately?"

He jumped out of the chair. His book fell to the floor and slammed shut with a loud clap that attracted attention from all directions.

I ducked my head and heard him murmuring his apologies as he picked up the book and set it on the table.

"What are you doing here?" he whispered.

"I thought I would check around and remember what life was like before it turned into something from a TV show," I whispered back.

"What's that supposed to mean?"

"Since when do you sound so nasty with me? I thought you'd be happy to see me after all this time."

"Yeah, all this time with no idea where you were or what you were doing. I mean, come on, Anissa. I thought we were closer than that." He glanced around to be sure we weren't overheard.

I did the same.

"We are closer than that, but there's been so much. I'm sorry. I wish there was a way I could keep in touch with you while this is happening, but it's for the best you don't know much about it. Trust me. You're better off where you are now."

He rolled his eyes. "Yeah, okay. Easy for you to say. Meanwhile, I have to wonder where my friend is and if she's alive."

"I'm sorry. I really am." I reached for him and was startled when he pulled away.

He ran a hand through his hair. "I'm sorry. But you can't come strolling back in and act like nothing's wrong. I mean, after you ran off with *him*."

Him.

So that was what this was all about.

I let out a soft sigh. "You mean Jonah."

"Who else? You chose him and his clan over... over us." He stopped himself short, but I knew what he meant.

I chose Jonah over him. I knew it would come to this one day, that just being friends wouldn't be enough for him after a while.

It was inconvenient he chose this very moment to hurl it in my face.

"It's a long story—nothing I can get into right now. You deserve to know everything. But now isn't the time. I'm sorry,

233

Raze. I wish I could tell you more, but I can't." I leaned against the chair, suddenly very tired. "I wish I had somebody I could pour this all out to. You have no idea."

He was quiet for a while. Then, "What's with your face?" He reached out to touch my skin. I flinched, and he pulled away.

"Sorry. It's not you. It's that they're not healed yet." I turned my face away to hide the worst of the scarring. It would be a little more time before my skin fully healed from being exposed to sunlight.

"What happened to you?"

"Like I said, long story. I'm all right now. Believe me, okay?"

"Right." He folded his thick arms. "You can't tell me what you've been doing, and I'm sure you're gonna tell me you can't stay around. Why are you here, then? What do you want from me?"

I hoped there would come a day when he wasn't so angry with me. I told myself there would be a time when we could talk it all out. I could tell him everything then.

"You're right. I need your help."

"I thought so. You can't tell me what you're doing, but you can ask me for help."

"Because you're the only one who can do this for me. Please. I need you." I forced myself to hold eye contact though he looked at me with hurt and disgust.

I hated to see him this way.

Then his shoulders slumped a little. "What do you need?"

Hope flickered in my chest. "I need you to go back to the mansion and into my rooms. There's a wardrobe in my bedroom. Behind the clothes, there's a hidden opening." I told him how to access it. "There's a shelf where I store my back-pack. It has everything I need in it. Please. Can you bring it to me?"

"I guess so. You want it here?"

"Yeah, if you can. I guess I'm safe enough here for a while."

"It'll probably take a couple of hours. I can't simply walk in, take it, and walk back out. You know how it is. I don't want anybody following me."

Yes, I knew how it was. Marcus would be tighter than ever when it came to security.

"Okay. I'll be here. Please, hurry if you can." There was so much to do.

He would never understand how desperate I was at that moment.

All he did was nod and turn away, book forgotten.

I decided to flip through his book in the meantime. A history of the city. He was always fascinated with history.

I skimmed the pages—my thoughts elsewhere. The pictures of the men and women in horse-drawn carriages made me think of the early days of the clan, and my parents. I remembered the story my father told about how he met my mother and the happy times they spent together.

Granted, they weren't taking carriages everywhere, but they walked through the park and saw change taking place all around them through the time they were together.

Would it be the same for Jonah and me? Would we ever have time to be happy together?

No sooner did I have that thought than I became angry all over again. Jonah had pushed me away.

I flipped the page and decided to keep those thoughts at bay.

❧

I FELT RAZE'S PRESENCE BEFORE I SAW HIM; I COULD SENSE HIM walking toward me. I looked up and almost cheered when I noted my backpack over his shoulder.

"Thank you, thank you, thank you a million times," I whispered as I took it with shaking hands.

"No problem. At least I did something to help you."

My heart sank a little. "I really am sorry. I mean it." I touched his arm.

"Yeah, well, as long as you're taking care of yourself."

"I'm trying to. This will help," I said as I lifted the pack onto my back. "Hey, you haven't seen my sister, have you? Or heard anything about her?"

"No. What, you don't know where she is?"

"It isn't that. I was only wondering if you'd heard rumors, that sort of thing."

He shook his head. "Nah. I mean, nothing worth paying attention to. You know how people talk. I figured she was with you."

"Yes and no." I'd find her back at Jonah's place. I bit back a sigh. And hopefully not run into him. Though a part of me wanted to. Then again, another part of me wanted to punch him for abandoning me with my father in Avellane.

It was better to leave it there with Raze. I stood on tiptoe to give him a peck on the cheek.

He gave me a sad little half-smile when I stepped back.

"I've gotta go." I squeezed his arm once before hurrying off, yanking the hood over my head again, prior to going back into the darkness.

The mist had stopped, and the air was dry. Good thing, too, since I needed to use the tools in my backpack and couldn't do it easily in the rain.

In minutes, I made it to a building a couple of blocks from the Bourke clan high-rise. Was Jonah up there? My heart raced at the thought, but this wasn't the time.

I had work to do, so I pulled out the special boots and gloves I used for climbing and pulled them on in the darkness between the two buildings before I started my climb to the top. The special rubber I wore created a suction effect, letting me grip even the slickest of surfaces. It was forty floors to the top, and I made the trip in just a few minutes—not as convenient as an elevator, but I couldn't have everything.

Once I made it to the roof of the building, I made a plan for how I'd get to the Bourke roof. I needed several lengths of cable and the grappling hook, so I pulled them from the pack along with my trusty silver blade and sheath.

It felt right, tightening the leather holster around my waist. I slid another, thicker blade in there alongside the first. Just in case. I didn't feel so naked anymore, once I had my weapons securely in place.

The backpack would be safe in a tight space between two air duct vents, so I stashed it there before getting ready to make my sojourn. I'd be crossing high above two busy streets to get to where Jonah's clan lived.

Not like this was my first time, but I could never calm the rush of adrenaline just before I prepared to swing the rope above my head and toss the hook to the next building. There was always a chance the hook wouldn't catch or the cable would snap. Then where would I be?

A grim smile made its way to my lips, perhaps in defiance of the situation.

As always, the hook caught on the lip around the building's roof. I pulled it to be sure it was tight then latched my handgrips to the cable and held on as I kicked off the edge of the roof to glide to the other side. It was as close as I would ever get to flying.

I repeated the process to get to Jonah's building. Most of the windows were dark, making me wonder where the clan was. Usually, all lights were blazing away.

Fewer eyes on me, I told myself as I glided across to the rooftop.

I tucked the hook and grips in a dark corner. The roof was empty, the wind whipping through my hood and roaring in my ears. I was about to slip through the glass doors to the penthouse to do a little snooping when a portal opened.

Out of freaking nowhere, a freaking portal. Damn the luck.

I looked around, frantic, then ducked behind the chimney just before two figures stepped out.

I held my breath.

One of them was tall, with broad shoulders and a muscular build. His deep-auburn hair caught my eye.

Behind him was Jonah.

My breath hitched this time. I hoped I hadn't made a sound that preternatural ears could capture.

It took every bit of self-control not to scream Jonah's name.

He was safe, for the time being.

That had to be enough for me. If I could only touch him, hold him for a second. My arms ached for him.

But no. I couldn't let the other vampire know I was here. He was a powerful one, too, based on the aura around him.

It was stronger than any I had ever seen, and almost pure, deep indigo.

Who was he?

I bit back a gasp.

Could it be Fane? It all fit. A powerful vampire traveling with Jonah. But why were they still traveling together?

They exchanged a few words before Jonah left him alone, vanishing into the stairwell.

The powerful vampire paced back and forth with his hands behind his back, muttering to himself.

As though he was nervous, almost.

Fane? Nervous? Over what? Maybe it wasn't Fane, after all. Fane wasn't afraid of anything, or so the legends said.

Minutes passed before Jonah reappeared with Philippa.

To my surprise, she threw herself at the vampire, arms around his neck. Who was he, and why was she acting that way? He pulled himself away from her. Things got heated—of course they did, with her involved.

I couldn't help smirking a little. She seemed to be telling them both off, but I couldn't pick up a single word, not even with my vampire super-hearing, thanks to the wind blowing it all away.

Suddenly, all three of them moved into the shadows of the other side of the chimney I was hiding behind.

I held my breath, frozen in place.

What would they think if they found me spying?

Not that I'd meant to. It wasn't my fault they showed up as I got there.

Philippa stormed off into the penthouse, leaving Jonah and the other vampire on their own.

What a surprise, she was upset about something.

Jonah acted as though he wanted to follow her, which of course was what she wanted because she loved attention so much.

The other vampire threw a portal.

No!

I didn't want to lose Jonah again so easily. I wanted to jump out and tell him not to leave me. But I couldn't.

I had to watch while he stepped through the portal.

It closed right away, and, in seconds, it was like there had never been one at all.

I was alone again.

I hope you enjoyed *Sanctuary*! I can't wait to bring you the next
book in this series!
Absolution

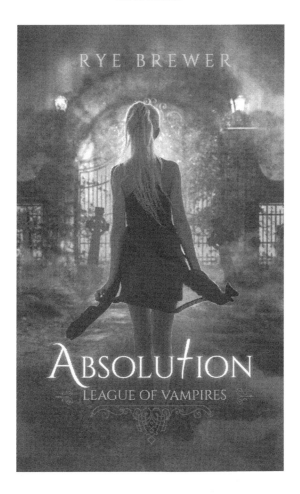

Sign up for the newsletter to be notified of new releases.

For Rye's website, put the following in a browser window:
www.leagueofvampires.com

To sign up for Rye's newsletter, put this in a browser window:
mailerlite.com/webforms/landing/k9z2k8

68954517R00146

Made in the USA
Middletown, DE
03 April 2018